The
DOLL
People

DOLL HOUSES

26117. Solid wood. One of our most popular designs. Brick details. Façade open door. Price.....$10.00

26118. High quality. Front-opening doll house with brass hinges. Two chimneys. Eight rooms. Heart-shaped lock keeps dolls securely inside.

Price.....$13.00

26119. Shingled doll house with enclosed porch. Price.....$15.00

AUNT DOLLS

26120. Pink bows with brilliantly decorated hat. The costume is a work of art, made of the finest silk with lace trim. Ivory buttons. Best aunt dolls available anywhere! Price.....$2.00

26121. Same: with violet coat and flowing hair......$2.75

DOLL FURNITURE

26122. Made of hardwood with handsome carved back. This chair comes with oak table with turned legs.
Price.....$1.00

KITCHEN SUPPLIES

26126. Tin kitchen set. Small size. Price.....$0.20

UNCLE DOLLS

26123. Bisque head. Tweed suit. Price.....$1.50

26124. Same as above with shiny gold watch chain. Price.....$1.75

26125. Same as above with striped suit and silk top hat. Price.....$1.85

DOLL SUNDRIES

26127. Doll hats. Assorted sizes. Price per pair....$0.10

26128. Doll bootie. Crocheted in wool. Price per pair.....$0.

26129. Doll embroidered silk coat. Each.....$0.40

WILSON & SONS CATALOGUE No. 61

BABY DOLLS
ASSORTED SIZES

26130. Full-jointed dolls. Finest bisque head. Long baby dress. Price.....$0.85

131. Superior quality lls with bisque heads, wool ess. Price.....$0.75

26132. Fine lace dress with silk bow. Price.....$0.50

133. Large baby ll. Full bonnet th lace trim. sque head. ice.....$1.00

134. Fine th body, ple bonnet. ice.....$0.70

PAPA DOLLS

26135. Dressed doll with bisque head and limbs. Finest checkered suit. Height: four inches. Price.....$1.25

26136. Same as above with top hat and overcoat. Price.....$2.00

MAMA DOLLS

26137. Finest muslin and lace dress. Bisque head with painted hair. Smooth finish. Bisque hands and legs. Price.....$1.50

26138. Other mama dolls with various styles in dresses and hair. Price.....$1.50 each

GIRL DOLLS

26139. Our most popular doll. Fine pink ribbon and painted yellow hair. Full lace sleeves and undertrimmings. Price.....$1.00

26140. Same as above, but with pink party outfit and yellow toy balloon. Price.....$1.25

BOY DOLLS

26141. Bisque head and limbs with fashionable sailor suit. Price.....$0.95

TINY BOOKS

26142. real bindings. Many titles. Set of ten Price.....$0.75

(kindly cut along the dotted line)

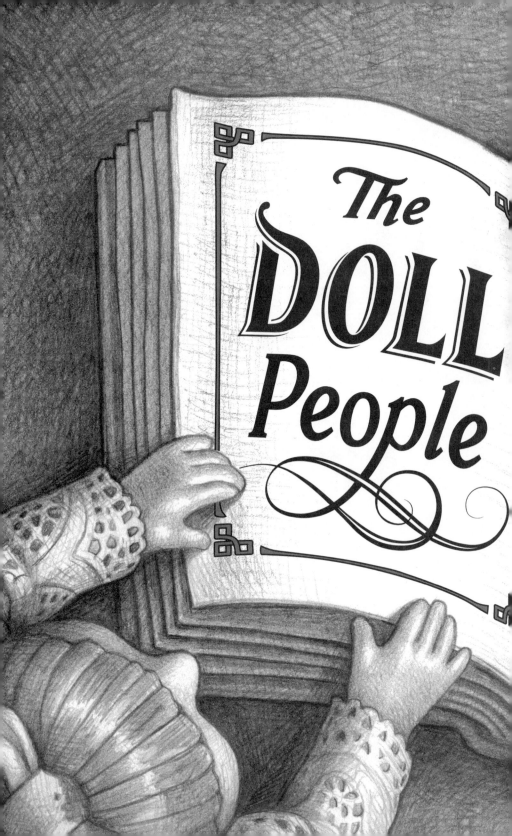

Ann M. Martin
and
Laura Godwin

with pictures by
Brian Selznick

◆

Hyperion Paperbacks
for Children
New York

Brian would like to thank the staff at Crush in Brooklyn, New York.

Text copyright © 2000 by Ann M. Martin and Laura Godwin
Illustrations copyright © 2000 by Brian Selznick

First Hyperion Paperback edition, 2002
5 7 9 10 8 6 4
Handlettering by Alex Ferrari based on design by Brian Selznick
Book design by Brian Selznick and Christine Kettner
Printed in the United States of America

Visit www.hyperionchildrensbooks.com

LIBRARY OF CONGRESS CATALOGING-IN-PUBLICATION DATA
Martin, Ann M., 1955—
The doll people / by Ann M. Martin and Laura Godwin ;
illustrated by Brian Selznick.—1st ed.
p.   cm.
Summary: A family of porcelain dolls that has lived in the same house for one hundred years is taken aback when a new family of plastic dolls arrives and doesn't follow The Doll Code of Honor.
ISBN 0-7868-0361-4 (trade) — ISBN 0-7868-2372-0 (lib. ed.)
ISBN 0-7868-1240-0 (pbk. ed.)
[1. Dolls— Fiction.] I. Godwin, Laura.
II. Selznick, Brian, ill. III. Title.
PZ7.M3567585Do 2000
[Fic]— dc21
98-12344
CIP

For Kate and James
and for all our nieces and nephews:
Brett
Nora
Katelyn
Jenna
Rachel
Ben
Henry
Jonah
—A.M.M. and L.G.

For my nephews:
Brennan
Dillan
—B.S.

Contents

Prologue / 1

1. Annabelle Doll's Secret / 5

2. The Mystery of Auntie Sarah / 17

3. Where Could She Be? / 31

4. Hello, Funcrafts / 44

5. The Funcrafts Come Visiting / 57

6. Annabelle Downstairs / 73

7. Doll State / 89

8. SELMP / 99

9. Exploring / 110

10. Uncle Doll Moves Out / 123

11. The Attic / 136

12. The Dolls Go Visiting / 146

13. Where's Papa? / 158

14. The Funcrafts to the Rescue / 176

15. Into the Attic / 191

16. The Dolls Make a Plan / 207

17. The Captain Helps Out / 223

18. Annabelle's Birthday Party / 234

19. Grandma Katherine and the Dolls / 252

*I*T HAD BEEN FORTY-FIVE years since Annabelle Doll had last seen Auntie Sarah. And forty-five years is a very long time, especially for an eight-year-old girl.

The dollhouse, where Annabelle lived with her family, hadn't changed much over these years. True, tiny things had been added or had been broken or lost. A rug that had lain on the floor under the dollhouse had been taken away and never replaced. Panes of glass had fallen out of some of the windows in the dollhouse, and the wallpaper in the kitchen had been painted over. But those were small changes.

The Dolls themselves had remained much the same, as well. Their china skin was a bit grayer, and their clothes were a bit more frayed, but otherwise they looked almost the same as they had the day Auntie Sarah was lost. In fact, the Dolls looked very much the same as they had the day they first arrived at 26 Wetherby Lane. However, they had once been a family of eight (if you included, as the Dolls did, the children's nanny as a member of the family), and now they were a family of seven.

Outside the dollhouse, in Kate's room and beyond, everything changed. Little girls grew up and had little girls of their own, people left the house and went to work or on vacations. History was made. Things happened. But inside the dollhouse, not much happened, as far as Annabelle was concerned. The only important event in her entire, one-hundred-year life was that Auntie Sarah had disappeared.

But today, the second most important event had occurred: Annabelle had found something that had belonged to Auntie

Sarah. No one knew she had found it. Not Kate Palmer. Not any of the Dolls. And keeping a secret in a house like Annabelle's was awfully hard. It might even be impossible, Annabelle thought, except for the fact that there was no one with whom Annabelle wanted to share a secret.

CHAPTER ONE

Annabelle Doll's Secret

NNABELLE looked around the dollhouse nursery, feeling restless. "Bobby," she said to her brother, "let's play tag."

Bobby Doll was propped up in a corner by the stairway landing in the dollhouse. That was where Kate Palmer had left him before school that morning.

"Do you think that's safe, Annabelle?" asked Bobby. "The Captain is right outside."

Annabelle didn't have a chance to answer his question. "No, it's not safe!" Mama Doll called from downstairs. Mama was standing

on her head next to the piano, which was
where Kate had left *her* that morning. It was a
most uncomfortable position. "If you move
around now, Kate might come home and see
you. And Bobby's right. The Captain is just
outside."

Annabelle looked out
the side window of
the dollhouse
and saw the
round yellow
eye of a cat
staring back at
her. She sighed.
Why couldn't
The Captain
take a
nap?

Annabelle flopped on her bed. She tried to remember where Kate had left her that morning. It had been somewhere in the nursery. On her bed? Sitting on the floor playing with Baby Betsy? Calling to Nanny from the doorway? Annabelle got to her feet again and peered through the window. The Captain was still standing on the shelf on which the dollhouse sat, staring in at the Dolls. When he saw Annabelle he licked his lips. Annabelle stuck her tongue out at him.

"Scat!" she called in her tiny doll voice.

"Annabelle, hush!" said Nanny.

Annabelle couldn't see Nanny, but she pushed herself away from the window anyway.

"This is so boring," she exclaimed. "My *life* is so boring."

No one answered her.

"Kate won't be home from school for ages!" she went on.

Silence.

I am going to die from boredom, thought Annabelle. She flopped on her bed again. "Mama, can I ask you a question?" she called out.

"Is it a quick question?"

"I want to know how Auntie Sarah is related to us. Is she your sister, or is she Papa's? Or is Uncle Doll your brother and—"

"Annabelle, that is not a quick question," called Papa Doll from somewhere.

And at that moment, Annabelle heard the Palmers' front door slam, heard Kate shout, "I'm home!," heard feet clattering on the stairs. The feet were somewhere near the top of the staircase when Annabelle remembered just where Kate had left her that morning. In a flash, Annabelle scooted across the nursery, and landed on Bobby's bed. By the time Kate ran into her room, Annabelle was propped against the head-board, her legs sticking out in front of her, her painted eyes staring ahead.

For the next three hours, while Kate did her third-grade homework, telephoned her friend Rachel, and tried to keep her little sister, Nora, out of her room, Annabelle sat on Bobby's bed and thought about her secret. Her secret was wonderful, and it was the only thing, the *only* thing, that prevented Annabelle from actually dying of boredom.

Annabelle recalled the moment when she had made her discovery. It had been during a night when Kate had closed the front of the dollhouse before she had gone to bed. She rarely did this, and when she did, Annabelle was delighted. It meant the Dolls had plenty of privacy during their nighttime, the time when the humans slept and the Doll family could move about their house. They could be a teeny bit less quiet, a teeny bit more free. Even The Captain, who usually snoozed at the end of Kate's bed, couldn't harm them.

And since they would have more freedom than usual on that night, Mama Doll had said, "How about a sing-along, and then free time?"

"Yes!" Annabelle had cried. Sing-alongs were always fun, and free time meant time when the Dolls could go anywhere in their house, and do anything they wanted to do,

9

within reason. "Remember," Papa often said, "never do anything you can't *undo* by the time Kate wakes up in the morning."

The Dolls had gathered around the piano in the parlor. Uncle Doll propped two songbooks in front of him. One was a book of hymns. It had come from England a hundred years earlier with the Dolls and the house and the furniture. The other book had been purchased by Mrs. Palmer, Kate's mother, when she was a young girl and the dollhouse had been hers. On the cover of the book was a rainbow. Written across the yellow band of the rainbow were the words GREAT HITS OF THE SIXTIES.

"Let's sing 'Natural Woman,'" Annabelle had suggested.

"Yuck," said Bobby.

"Okay, then 'Respect,'" said Annabelle.

"R-E-S-P-E-C-T!" sang Bobby.

"Sockittome, sockittome, sockittome, sockittome!" Annabelle chimed in.

"How about a quieter song?" suggested Nanny.

The Dolls had sung song after song while Uncle Doll played the piano. Outside the dollhouse, Annabelle caught a glimpse of The Captain. He sat silently on Kate's bed, listening to the doll voices. He could barely hear them, but they were there, all right. The Dolls ended the singalong after two choruses of "Bringing in the Sheaves" from the hymnbook. And then their free time began. Annabelle knew exactly what she was going to do. She wanted to examine the books in the library. And she wanted to do it privately. Lately, Kate and Rachel had talked of nothing but Nancy Drew and how she solved her mysteries. They had even read a couple of the mysteries aloud to each other, and Annabelle had listened intently. She wished she could be a detective like Nancy. And now she thought she might find something interesting on the dollhouse bookshelves. It was unlikely. But possible. Annabelle knew that most of the books on the shelves were not real. They were simply flat blocks painted bright colors, with book titles written on one side in gold ink. But perhaps she might find a secret compartment in one of the shelves. Things like that were always happening to Nancy.

So, in the glow of Kate's night-light, Annabelle had begun her search. She started by removing the books from the shelves, one by one. Presently she discovered that some of the books were attached to one another. She could remove a whole block of books at once. This was interesting, but not very mysterious. Then she discovered that some of the books were, in fact, real, like the songbooks. She could open their covers and inside were a few pages with crowded writing: *Classics of Modern Poetry, Oliver Twist*. Annabelle read the twenty-page story about the little

boy named Oliver with great interest.
Eagerly, she pulled out every book from the
shelves. But the others were pretend. She
checked for secret compartments. Nothing.
She stood on a stool and tackled the next
shelf. Only pretend books. She stood on
tiptoe and reached for the shelf above. And
that was where she found Auntie Sarah's
journal.

From the outside it looked like all the other
books on the shelves. It was dark green, with
gold writing stamped on the cover. The title
was *My Journal*. It was fatter than most of the
books, though, and contained dozens of
pages as thin as onionskin, filled with spidery
black handwriting and even
some drawings.

    Annabelle
stepped off of the
stool and sat on the
floor to look through
My Journal. She
opened to the first
page. And there
she found the words

"The Private Diary of Sarah Doll, May 1955."

Sarah Doll. That must be Auntie Sarah, Annabelle had thought. She gasped. And when she heard the voices of Mama and Papa on the staircase she had shoved the book under the hem of her long dress.

"Annabelle," Mama had said, "let's have a bit of family time while we can still talk freely, and then we will have to go back to our places. Kate will be up soon."

"All right," replied Annabelle. She had managed to scurry upstairs without anyone's seeing the book, and she had hidden it under the covers of her bed. She knew that was dangerous. What if Kate, of all people, should find the book there while she was playing in the dollhouse? But Annabelle couldn't help herself.

For the last week she had read the book in snatches, whenever Kate was gone or asleep, and Annabelle's family was in other rooms. Each time she read a few more pages she would close the book and once again place it under the covers, feeling restless. Annabelle was used to feeling bored. But not restless. Something

was wrong with her life. Something was missing. It wasn't anything specific such as a hair-
brush or a shoe. Annabelle didn't even think it
was Auntie Sarah. Not exactly. It was . . . what
was it? Was it possible to miss something you
had never had?

Annabelle now sat stiffly on Bobby's bed,
waiting for Kate to be called downstairs for
supper. She thought about the last time the
Dolls had seen Auntie Sarah. Annabelle
remembered it as a day like any other, except
that one moment Auntie Sarah was in the
parlor, and the next moment she wasn't. And
she hadn't been seen since.

Annabelle thought again about Auntie
Sarah's journal. Many of the pages were filled
with drawings, mainly drawings of spiders. In
some of the drawings Auntie Sarah had even
labeled the parts of the spiders. Annabelle had
read just a few of the pages of words, and this
had taken her a long time because Auntie
Sarah's crawly handwriting was hard to read.
All Annabelle had learned so far was that daily
life in 1955 had barely been different from
Annabelle's life today.

Annabelle let out a sigh, hoping Kate wouldn't hear her. If Kate had a secret, Annabelle thought, whom would she tell it to?

CHAPTER TWO

The Mystery of Auntie Sarah

HILE LATE NIGHT was the Dolls' very best time, the morning wasn't bad. By nine o'clock on most days, Mr. and Mrs. Palmer had left for their jobs, Kate had left for school, and Grandma Katherine had taken Nora to preschool. Often Grandma Katherine ran errands after that, so the Dolls had some time to themselves. One Wednesday, exactly a week after she had found Auntie Sarah's journal, Annabelle was lying on the floor of the nursery drawing pictures of spiders when she heard the Palmers' clock chime noon.

"Noon!" exclaimed Annabelle. She had lost track of time. Just as she was shoving her papers under her bed she heard voices from downstairs.

"Nora's home," Mama said in a loud voice. "Places, everyone."

Annabelle tossed herself on the floor where Kate had left her the night before. A moment later, Nora was standing on the stool in front of the Dolls' house, her hands on her hips. She peered inside. Kate had not closed the front of the house, so Nora reached in.

"Hum, hum, de-hum," she sang softly. "Look, Captain. Look what Kate's dollies can do." (The Captain, sleeping in his spot on Kate's bed, didn't stir.)

Nora picked up Bobby. She bounced him down the stairs. "Boink, boink, boink," she said. She flew him out of the house, and into the Dolls' kitchen, opened the front of the old-fashioned icebox, and stuffed him inside. Then she picked up Baby Betsy and tried to stuff her inside. "Uh-oh, Baby Betsy. Your head is too big. You do not fit." Nora left Baby Betsy on the kitchen floor. She put Uncle Doll in the icebox with Bobby. And

then she bounced Annabelle down the stairs. "Boink, boink, boink. Okay, Annabelle. Come into the kitchen for a surprise." Nora bounced Annabelle through the dining room and into the kitchen. "Open the icebox, Annabelle. . . . Look! Look inside. The dollies are in the icebox. How did they get in there?"

Nora regarded the Dolls. "You dollies have no pets," she said. "No pets at all. How sad. You need some pets. I know! Rancher Family!"

Nora tossed Annabelle and Bobby back into the nursery, then ran from the room.

No, no, no, thought Annabelle. Not Rancher Family.

Nora was running back into Kate's room carrying a pail full of plastic farm animals when Annabelle dared to turn around and glance at Bobby. He was rolling under his bed.

"Bobby," hissed Nanny from her room. But she could say no more. Nora would hear her.

"Here we go, Rancher Family," said Nora, reaching into the pail. She set two cows and one of her horses in the parlor of the dollhouse. Then she grabbed Annabelle, Nanny, and Uncle Doll, and sat Annabelle and Uncle Doll on the cows, and Nanny on the horse.

"Ride 'em, cowboys!" called Nora. "Now it's time for the roundup. Yippee-ki-yo-ki-yay! Gallop, gallop." Nora made the cows and the horse gallop from the parlor, through the dining room, into the kitchen, and back to the parlor.

Oh, thought Annabelle, this is disgusting. I am sitting on Nora's dirty old cow. She looked at a gray wad of formerly pink bubble gum dangling from one of its ears. The cow wobbled on three legs, since the fourth was shorter and badly misshapen, sporting tiny rows of teeth marks from above the knee down to the hoof. While Annabelle perched

precariously on her cow, she stole a glance at Nanny. Nanny had always said that having animals in the house was unseemly. And Annabelle knew why. All of Nora's animals were slimy and grimy and gray, and who knew where they'd been.

Annabelle sat miserably on the back of the cow. Oh, please, oh, please. Someone save me, she thought.

And at that moment she heard a voice call from downstairs, "Nora! Lunchtime!"

"Okay!" Nora replied. She scooped most of her animals back into their bucket. But she left two dusty chickens behind. And she left Nanny on the horse, and Annabelle and Uncle Doll on the cows.

Annabelle sat on her cow and waited. She tried not to look at the cow. Disgusting, disgusting, she thought.

After two or three minutes Annabelle couldn't stand it any longer. She swung her leg over the back of the cow and began to slide down its side.

"Annabelle," said Mama warningly from her chair in the kitchen.

"Mama, I *have* to get off of this cow."

"Honey, what if Nora returns and sees you moving? Do you want to wind up in Doll State?"

Doll State. Annabelle had been in Doll State several times, more often than anyone else in her family. It was so unfair. A human saw her moving, or thought he saw her moving, and bang, just like that, Annabelle was rendered an ordinary doll, a doll who couldn't move. But only for twenty-four hours, she reminded herself. Just for one day.

Annabelle slid a bit farther off of the cow.

"Annabelle," said Nanny, "there is good reason for Doll State. Just think what would happen if humans discovered that some dolls are alive. Why, we would never be left alone."

"I know, I know. We would be put on display like people in a circus sideshow. Or studied like lab animals," said Annabelle, who had heard this a thousand times before.

"And if you take too big a risk—if you do something that truly jeopardizes dollkind—you could enter Permanent Doll State. And become an ordinary doll forever."

Annabelle stole a glance at Bobby. The adults were always threatening her and Bobby with Permanent Doll State, but Annabelle didn't believe it existed. For one thing, no one had been very clear about what, exactly, caused Permanent Doll State. Even so, Annabelle straightened herself up and sat tall on the cow again.

"Thank you, Annabelle," said Nanny.

Annabelle tried not to look at the cow. "Mama," she said, "if we have to be stuck here until Kate comes home and rescues us, can we at least talk? Please tell me about when we left

England and came to the Palmers' house."

Mama smiled. "Honey, you know that story by heart. Besides, you were there when it happened."

"I know, but I like to hear you tell it."

"Well . . . all right. Uncle Doll, you keep your eyes and ears open and let us know right away if anyone is coming."

Uncle Doll, who was facing the doorway to Kate's room, nodded his head. "Okay," he said.

Mama folded her hands in her lap. "It all began over one hundred years ago, in eighteen ninety-eight," she said, "when William Seaborn Cox wanted to buy a special gift for his newborn daughter, Gertrude. So he sent to England for a large dollhouse, completely furnished, and a set of dolls."

"That's us, right, Mama?" said Bobby.

"Yes, that's right," agreed Mama. "Several months later the dollhouse arrived at a port in the United States after a long journey across the ocean. Presently, it was delivered to Twenty-six Wetherby Lane—"

"And we stayed still as stone in our shipping box while William and his wife, Clara, unpacked the house and set it up in a corner of Gertrude's nursery," Annabelle chimed in. "And we've lived here ever since."

Mama smiled. "The end," she said.

"No, no! That's not the end," exclaimed Annabelle. "Tell the rest."

"Well, in a very short time, Gertrude grew up and had a daughter who played with us."

"That's Grandma Katherine," said Bobby.

"Yes. And when *she* grew up, *her* daughter played with us."

"That's Annie, Kate's mother," said Bobby.

"And now Kate plays with us."

"And she loves us every bit as much as Gertrude did," said Annabelle. "Okay, now tell about Baby Betsy."

"Well," Mama began, "when William and Clara first unpacked us they discovered that someone had made a mistake. The baby doll was very big, bigger even than you, Annabelle. She must have come from a different doll set. *We* didn't mind, of course. We already loved Baby Betsy very much. But Clara wondered at first what to do with this doll who was far too big to fit in her pram, whose arms stuck over the sides, and whose legs hung over the end. But she decided to keep her, and we were very relieved. We knew Baby Betsy was meant to be ours."

"And you don't mind if it takes you and Papa together to lift her," added Bobby.

"Not a bit," said Mama.

"Mama, tell us how many dolls William and Clara unpacked when our house arrived," said Annabelle.

"You know the answer to that perfectly well," Papa called from the other room.

"Mama?" said Annabelle.

Mama sighed. "Eight dolls."

"Eight," Annabelle repeated. "You and Papa, Nanny, Bobby, Baby Betsy, me, Uncle Doll, and . . ."

"And Auntie Sarah," replied Mama.

"And Auntie Sarah was with us until nineteen fifty-five," Annabelle went on. "Then one day . . ."

"She disappeared," said Mama uncomfortably.

"Mama, Papa, dolls don't just 'disappear,'" said Annabelle. "Something has to happen to them. Why won't you talk about Auntie Sarah? Don't you care what happened to her?"

Uncle Doll spoke up. "Of course we care, Annabelle," he said. "We care deeply."

Annabelle heard a catch in her uncle's voice. "But why doesn't anyone ever talk about that day?"

"What day, honey?" said Mama.

"The day she disappeared."

"There's nothing to say," Uncle Doll replied stiffly.

Annabelle thought about Auntie Sarah's secret journal. And she thought she knew better. She also knew it was time to stop talking about Auntie Sarah.

Annabelle thanked her mother for the story. Then she sat quietly on the cow until Kate returned from school. The moment Kate saw the plastic animals in the dollhouse she complained loudly to Grandma Katherine. "Nora won't leave my things alone. I will be so glad when it's her birthday." Annabelle wondered what that meant, exactly, while Kate rescued the Dolls and sat them in the parlor for tea.

Late that night, when Kate was asleep and The Captain was perched on the end of her bed staring into the open dollhouse, Annabelle turned to her mother and said, "Thank goodness for Kate. She always rescues us, doesn't she? I think Kate is my best friend."

"Kate is a lovely little girl," Mama replied gently, "but I'm not sure that little girl humans are the best friends for little girl dolls."

Annabelle thought this over. "Because she's going to grow up and I'm not? Is that right?"

"Yes."

"Hmm," said Annabelle. "Well, then . . ." She could think of no way to finish her sentence. And later, curled up on her bed alone in the nursery, Annabelle hugged the secret of Auntie Sarah to herself.

CHAPTER THREE

Where Could She Be?

ONE SATURDAY, Annabelle sat at the table in the Dolls' kitchen, gazing ahead of her. Kate and Rachel were sprawled on Kate's bed, discussing the clues to a Nancy Drew mystery. Annabelle wasn't listening to them. Her eyes were fixed on a large brown spider inching its way into the kitchen. Annabelle wanted to scream and run from the room. The spider was nearly as big as her head. And it was making its way toward Annabelle's chair. The spider couldn't bite Annabelle, of course, since she was made of china. But more than once a spider had crawled across

Annabelle, and she had had to sit still as the hairy legs crept over her arms, her face.

Please, please go in some other direction, Annabelle silently prayed. As the spider continued its journey toward her, she thought of Auntie Sarah and her drawings of spiders. Perhaps Auntie Sarah had liked spiders and insects. Annabelle hadn't been able to spend much time with the journal lately. She desperately wanted to read more of it. But only if she could do so privately.

The spider took two more steps toward Annabelle. Annabelle tried not to look at it. She imagined Auntie Sarah sitting in the dollhouse studying spiders, although she couldn't remember this actually happening. In fact, spiders and insects only occasionally crept into the house. Annabelle frowned. Something was wrong with the picture in her head.

Just two inches from Annabelle, the spider turned and began

making its way toward a window. Annabelle barely noticed. She couldn't stop thinking about Auntie Sarah and where, exactly, she had made her drawings.

That evening, Kate closed the front of the house firmly. Annabelle was thrilled. She knew exactly what she wanted to do with her free time that night, and as soon as she was able, she told her family she wanted some privacy, and settled on her bed in the nursery with Auntie Sarah's journal. This time Annabelle began to read it from the very beginning instead of skipping around, and she was able to read nearly twenty pages before Papa called, "Places, everyone."

The first few pages, on which Auntie Sarah recorded details of her everyday life in the dollhouse, were not of much interest, since the Dolls' lives then were nearly like they were today. Then Annabelle found an entry that began:

The time has come for another adventure. Tomorrow I set out for the living room. I plan to blend somewhere near the radio.

Annabelle paused. There was no radio in

the parlor of the Dolls' house. There never had been. And "blend"? What did that mean? Annabelle had heard the word before, of course, but never used in quite that way. Puzzled, she read on. A page later, Auntie Sarah wrote:

Hard to believe. Am writing this sitting on table in living room. Katherine and her husband were just here. Were talking about baby they are going to have. Now am listening to news. Huge storm expected tomorrow. Hurricane Connie. Very exciting.

Annabelle stopped reading again. Katherine and her husband were where? In Katherine's old bedroom? That didn't sound right to Annabelle, since Katherine had moved to a bedroom down the hall when she'd gotten married. Still, maybe they were talking about redecorating the room for the baby who would be born soon, for Annie. But where was the radio?

Hurricane Connie. The news. Something stirred in Annabelle's mind. Excitement. Names. Names Annabelle hadn't thought of in decades. Amelia Earhart. Eleanor Roosevelt. Auntie Sarah used to tell Annabelle about events in the news and

especially about women she admired. But how
had she known about them?

Had Auntie Sarah *left* the dollhouse? Was
it possible she was talking about the living
room of the *humans'* house? She had, after all,
written "living room," not "parlor."
Annabelle let the journal slip from her hands
and fall to the bed. This was nearly unthink-
able. The Dolls never left their house; not on
their own. Occasionally, they had been carried out of the house, most recently by Kate
and Nora, but they had never left it on their
own. It sat on a shelf several feet above the
floor. Even if a doll could leave the house,
could she run across the floor unseen?
Annabelle thought about Permanent Doll
State. Perhaps this was the sort of risk that
would lead to Permanent Doll State, the sort
of risk grown-ups had in mind but never
spoke of.

Annabelle's hands were trembling as she
picked up the journal again. The spiders. Had
Auntie Sarah left the house to study them?
Had she sneaked out into the world of
the humans, and somehow blended in with
them? Had she managed, unseen, to overhear

their conversations, to listen to their news on the radio? Maybe, just maybe, she had even read some of their books. It would have been a struggle to open them, but Annabelle had a feeling that Auntie Sarah might have been able to do it, to do all these things. She didn't know how Auntie Sarah had gone in and out of the dollhouse without Annabelle's seeing her. That was a mystery she would have to solve. But if what Annabelle was thinking were true, then perhaps Auntie Sarah wasn't missing after all. Perhaps she was somewhere in the Palmers' house.

* * *

The next morning, the moment Kate's house
had emptied, Annabelle said, "Mama, why
don't we ever leave our house?"

"Leave our house?" Mama repeated.
"Why, Annabelle, you know the answer to
that."

"I know you say it's because it isn't safe,"
Annabelle began.

"It most certainly is not," said Nanny.
"How would you leave the house anyway,
Annabelle?"

Annabelle, who was sitting on the floor
of the parlor with her legs dangling over the
edge, looked below her. It was a long way
down. The shelf on which the dollhouse sat

was in a corner of Kate's room. Just below it was the wooden stool. It was four steps high, painted white with pink roses. The top step was just two inches under the shelf. Kate used the stool to reach the rooms on the top floor of the house, although she no longer needed it for the rooms on the first floor. Sometimes she slid the stool under the shelf. But it was out now, and Annabelle studied it.

"I bet I could get down the steps of the stool," she said, leaning over.

"Oh, Annabelle," said Mama. "How would you get back up the steps? Each one is higher than you. And if you fell, you'd land on hard floor."

"You'd crack your head open," added Bobby.

"I just think I could do it. How did Auntie Sarah leave the house?" asked Annabelle.

For a moment, no one spoke. Annabelle looked intently at her parents.

"Annabelle," said Papa at last, "leaving the house is dangerous. The Captain—"

"You didn't answer my question,"

Annabelle persisted. "How did Auntie Sarah leave? I know she left."

"Oh, that was so long ago," said Mama. "Yes, she did used to leave, but . . . I have an idea. How about having a sing-along right now? It's a bit risky, but I think we can get away with it."

"What do you mean, Auntie Sarah used to leave the house?" interrupted Bobby.

"She did," said Annabelle. "All by herself."

"Is that true?" Bobby turned to Mama and Papa. "She really did?"

Mama and Papa glanced at each other, then at Uncle Doll. And Uncle Doll, to Annabelle's surprise, *glared* back at them.

"Why?" said Bobby. "Why did she do that? I mean, what did she do while she was out of the house? Where did she go? And, Annabelle, how do *you* know she used to do that?"

Everyone now turned to Annabelle.

Silence.

"Well, what about the sing-along?" said Mama brightly.

"We can start off with 'Respect,'" added Papa.

"No," said Annabelle. "I want to know

something. Didn't anybody ever look for Auntie Sarah after she disappeared?"

"Why, of course, Annabelle. We searched this house from top to bottom," replied Papa.

"But didn't you look for her outside of the house? Out . . . out there?" Annabelle gestured to Kate's room, and to the hallway beyond.

"Well, as we've said, that would have been very dangerous," said Papa.

"Hmphh." Uncle Doll turned his head away.

"But it was *Auntie Sarah*," said Annabelle, glancing curiously at her uncle. "If I were missing, wouldn't you look for me?"

"Goodness, Annabelle. I don't think you're going to go missing," said Nanny.

"I could. Something could happen to me and I could disappear and be in great danger. The Captain could climb up the stool and run off with me. Or Nora could take me and lose me somewhere. And I would hope you would look for me."

"But, Annabelle," said Nanny, "you know full well that that would put us in danger. We could wind up in Doll State or

Permanent Doll State."

"But after I was missing for *so long,* wouldn't you look for me? Mama? Papa? Wouldn't you?"

Mama and Papa looked at each other, then at Nanny. Uncle Doll glared at all three of them. No one said a word.

"How about 'Respect'?" suggested Bobby in a small voice.

Still no one said a word.

That night, long after Kate had gone to sleep and Mama had said it was all right to move about the house, Annabelle lay on her bed, refusing to speak to anyone. Her family left her alone, and she pulled Auntie Sarah's journal out from under her covers.

Annabelle skipped ahead a few pages and read that Auntie Sarah was planning a Nature Study Exploration. She squinted down at the fine pen marks on the page, frustrated at having to read such exciting words by Kate's night-light only.

I need to develop a greater understanding of the creatures in this house, Auntie Sarah had written. And Annabelle realized she meant the humans' house, not the Dolls' house.

Annabelle thought about this for a while. Then she snapped the journal shut, slid it under her covers, and marched out of the nursery and down the stairs to the parlor. There she found the rest of her family. The adults and Bobby were talking quietly while Baby Betsy sat leaning against the piano, playing with a stuffed bunny.

Annabelle stood still and looked at everybody, her hands on her hips. After a moment she said, "I have an announcement to make. I am going to search for Auntie Sarah."

Everyone began talking at once.

"Oh, no," said Mama.

"Annabelle, you can't," said Nanny.

"Right now?" asked Uncle Doll.

"That isn't safe," said Papa.

Annabelle thought about brave Auntie Sarah. She thought about Amelia Earhart and Eleanor Roosevelt and Nancy Drew. "I'm going anyway," she said.

The rest of the Dolls sat in

stunned silence. At last Uncle Doll rose to his feet. "Well, Annabelle, if you are going to go no matter what," he said slowly, "then I am going with you."

CHAPTER FOUR

Hello, Funcrafts

NNABELLE stared at her uncle. "You are?" she said at last.

"Yes."

"But why?"

"I just . . . am."

"Me, too," said Bobby.

Mama put her hand over her heart.

"I insist on only one thing," said Uncle Doll. "That we go tomorrow night. It's too late to leave now. The Palmers will be up soon. We must leave when we have plenty of time to get down the stool, and more important, to get back up the stool when we return."

And so it was settled. Mama, Papa, and Nanny were very frightened, but Uncle Doll had a private chat with them. Annabelle couldn't hear what he said to them, but when the chat was over, they agreed, unhappily, that Annabelle and Bobby could go with Uncle Doll.

Annabelle was jubilant. But how was she ever going to manage to wait during the whole long next day until the Palmers went to bed again? She did manage, of course, even though she was sure it was the most boring day of her entire life. The only vaguely interesting thing that happened was that just after lunchtime, a delivery truck pulled into the Palmers' driveway, the doorbell rang, and through Kate's open window Annabelle heard Grandma Katherine say to the delivery person, "Just in time. Her birthday is almost here. I have to hide this before she sees it." A moment later the front door closed. Not long after that, Annabelle heard Grandma Katherine come puffing up the stairs, heard a thud, the sound of another door opening, of something being slid along the floor, and of the door then being closed.

I bet Grandma Katherine just hid Nora's birthday present, Annabelle thought. And she spent quite a bit of the rest of the day wondering what the present could be.

By the time Kate went to bed that night, though, Annabelle had stopped thinking about the present. All she wanted was for Kate and the rest of the Palmers to fall asleep, and for deepest night to descend.

When it did, Annabelle ran to the front of the dollhouse and looked across Kate's room. She could just make out The Captain at the foot of Kate's bed.

"I think he's asleep," Annabelle whispered to Uncle Doll.

"I hope so," Uncle Doll replied nervously.

"Are you ready?" Annabelle asked Bobby and her uncle. They nodded. "Well, then, this is good-bye," said Annabelle to the rest of her family.

"Only for a few hours," said Bobby.

But Mama and Papa and Nanny looked as though they might never see the explorers again.

"We'll be back by four-thirty," promised Uncle Doll.

Mama swallowed hard.

Nanny turned away.

"Righto," said Papa.

Annabelle jumped from the parlor down to the stool. At the edge of the top step, she knelt, turned, and slid backward onto the next step, landing with a small thump. Bobby and Uncle Doll followed her. A few minutes later they were all sprawled in a heap on the floor.

Bobby glanced at Kate's bed. "Is she still asleep?" he asked.

"I think so," whispered Annabelle.

"Is The Captain still asleep?" asked Uncle Doll.

"I hope so," said Annabelle. "Let's go."

Uncle Doll hesitated.

"Oh, *please* don't change your mind. Think of Auntie Sarah. She needs us," whispered Annabelle.

Uncle Doll straightened himself. "Let's hurry, then," he said.

Annabelle led the way through the darkness across Kate's room.

They stopped at the doorway into the hall. Annabelle peered cautiously around it. "I don't see anything," she said. She stepped into the hall. It was very long and very dark.

"Did The Captain see us?" she asked Uncle Doll.

"I don't think so."

"Then let's start looking."

"Remember, we can't call for Auntie Sarah," said Uncle Doll. "Someone might hear us. All we can do is search."

Annabelle, Bobby, and Uncle Doll peered into the other rooms. They scooted under dressers and beds and armchairs. They peeked into closets and investigated shoes and slippers.

"If I were Auntie Sarah, I wonder where I would be," said Bobby after a while. "She must be up high. If she were down low the humans would have found her long ago."

"Unless she's really hidden," said Annabelle. "Inside something. In a box or a trunk. Or in a box in a trunk in a closet."

"I'm going to call for her anyway," said Bobby.

Uncle Doll grabbed his arm.

"I won't call loudly," said Bobby. "I'll just call like this: 'Auntie Sarahhhhhhh!' See? That's not so loud."

"I'll call, too," said Annabelle.

Annabelle, Bobby, and Uncle Doll were standing against a wall in a room with a couch and two chairs, but no bed.

"Whose room is this?" whispered Annabelle.

"I don't think it's a bedroom," replied Uncle Doll. "It looks like a sitting room."

"Good. We can call a little more loudly in here," said Bobby.

"Auntie Sarahhhhhhhhh!" Annabelle and Bobby called. "Auntie Sarahhhhhhh! Auntie Sarahhhhhhhh!"

"Hey," said Annabelle. "Did you hear something?"

"Yes. It sounded like a voice," exclaimed Uncle Doll. "Listen."

After a moment, Annabelle heard the voice again.

"Help!" it called. "Help! Help!"

And then, "Help!" cried another voice. "Help us."

"Uncle Doll," said Bobby, "does that sound like Auntie Sarah to you?"

Uncle Doll shook his head.

"If it's Auntie Sarah, she's with someone else," added Annabelle. She raised her voice slightly. "Auntie Sarah, is that you? Where are you?"

"We're over here. In this box," one of the voices replied.

"I think we're in a closet," another voice added. "But there's no one here named Auntie Sarah."

Annabelle spotted a closet door slightly ajar. "Come on," she said to Bobby and Uncle Doll.

Together they managed to swing the door open. By the moonlight streaming through a window, Annabelle could just make out a large cardboard carton with some letters and words printed on the sides.

"Hello?" said Annabelle.

"Hello?" replied a voice from inside the box.

"Who are you?" asked Annabelle.

"We are the Funcrafts. I'm Mom Funcraft."

"I'm Dad Funcraft," said a second voice.

"I'm Tiffany Funcraft. I'm the big sister."

"I'm Bailey Funcraft, the brother," said a younger-sounding voice.

"Baby Britney is here, too," said Mom Funcraft's voice. "But she's asleep."

"And anyway, she can't talk yet," added Tiffany.

"Who are you?" asked Dad Funcraft. "And who's Auntie Sarah?"

"I'm Annabelle Doll," said Annabelle, "and this is my brother, Bobby, and my uncle. Auntie Sarah is my aunt, Uncle Doll's wife. She's been missing for decades. We thought we would look for her tonight."

Annabelle's voice trailed off. She was trying to read the words on the side of the box. FUNCRAFT DOLL AND DREAM HOUSE SET MODEL IIO. INCLUDES PLASTIC DREAM HOUSE, DOLL FAMILY, ALL FURNITURE, AND SNAP-ON CLOTHES AND PARTS PICTURED ON FRONT. NOT RECOMMENDED FOR CHILDREN UNDER 3.

"Bobby! Uncle Doll!" said Annabelle in a loud whisper. "Another doll family is inside that box!"

"I wonder which doll maker made them, and how long it took them to travel across the ocean," said Bobby.

"I don't know. But let's see what's pictured on front," said Annabelle.

Annabelle, Bobby, and Uncle Doll scurried around to the other side of the carton. To Annabelle's dismay she discovered that the front was the side that had been placed on the floor.

"Rats," she exclaimed. "I wanted to see what they look like."

"Hello? Are you still out there?" called a voice. It sounded like Mom Funcraft's.

"Yes, we're here," said Annabelle. She paused. Then she called, "Did you come from England? How was your trip?"

"England?" repeated Mom Funcraft. "Is that a factory? That's where we came from. A factory in Cleveland."

"It was called Marwin, Inc.," Dad Funcraft volunteered. "Perhaps you've heard of it?"

"Marwin Ink Factory in Cleveland? No. . . . Where's Cleveland?" asked Uncle Doll.

"It's . . . it's, um . . . well . . ." said Dad Funcraft.

"Never mind," said Annabelle. "You know what? Our families are just the same. We each have a mother and a father, a big sister, a little brother, and a baby sister."

"I am *not* a little brother," said Bobby.

"Neither am I," said Bailey from inside the box.

"Plus," Bobby went on indignantly, "we have an uncle, an auntie, and Nanny."

"We have a cat," said Tiffany. "Her name is Kitty. Kitty Funcraft."

"A cat?" exclaimed Annabelle. "Is she alive?"

"Of course not," said Tiffany. "She's a toy animal."

Annabelle breathed a sigh of relief.

She wondered if Tiffany looked like her. Annabelle decided she did. All dollhouse dolls must look pretty much the same. Tiffany wouldn't have green paint on her head from a long-ago accident involving a paint box, as Annabelle did. And she would be clean and sparkly and new, her china skin smooth and uncracked, her clothes bright, not yet faded. But otherwise, Annabelle thought, she and Tiffany must look the same.

"When are your birthdays?" asked Annabelle.

"What kinds of toys do you have?" asked Bobby.

"Excuse me," said Mom Funcraft, "but before we answer your questions, do you think you could get us out of this box?"

"Goodness no!" cried Uncle Doll. "We couldn't do that. What would the Palmers think?"

"The Palmers?" repeated Dad Funcraft.

"This is their house," said Annabelle. "And we—my family and I— live in Kate Palmer's room. Kate is eight. She takes care of our dollhouse. I think you are going to be Nora's dolls. Nora is Kate's little sister."

Annabelle glanced at Bobby and Uncle Doll. She knew what they were thinking. It was just what Annabelle was thinking: *Those poor, poor Funcrafts. They have no idea what they're getting into. Nora's dolls . . . What a frightening thought. I hope they are strong. I hope they like farm animals.*

The Palmers' grandfather clock chimed then, and Uncle Doll took Annabelle's arm. "It's time to start heading back. It may take us a while to climb up the stool."

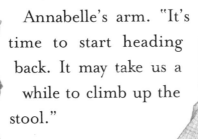

"We have to go now," Annabelle called to the Funcrafts.

"Oh, froggies!" said Tiffany. "You do?"

"Yes. But I don't think you're going to be stuck in this box for long. And as soon as you've been unpacked and set up in Nora's room we'll come visit you."

"Promise?" said Tiffany.

"Promise," replied Annabelle.

"We'll bring our whole family," added Bobby.

"All right," said Tiffany.

"It was nice meeting you," called Mom Funcraft.

"It was nice meeting *you*," Annabelle replied politely.

Then she and Bobby and Uncle Doll scooted out of the closet, through the sitting room, and down the dark hall to Kate's room. They hoisted themselves up the last step of the stool just as the clock chimed four-thirty.

CHAPTER FIVE

The Funcrafts Come Visiting

AMA! PAPA!"
said Annabelle breathlessly. "You'll never
guess what we found. Oh, we have so much to
tell you!"

"We found other dolls!" exclaimed
Bobby.

"No, *I* want to tell!" said Annabelle.

"You can't tell everything," said Bobby.

"Shh, shh," said Mama Doll softly. "I
think this should wait until later in the morning, when the Palmers are out."

"I can't wait that long," said Annabelle
desperately.

Kate stirred in her bed then, flung her arm over the side, and murmured something Annabelle couldn't understand.

Mama put her finger to her lips and shook her head. Then she pointed upstairs.

Places, everyone, thought Annabelle, and she headed for her bed, since Kate had carefully tucked the Dolls into bed the night before.

Hours later, when the last of the Palmers had left the house, Annabelle sprang out of her bed. "Okay!" she called. "Family meeting. Bobby and Uncle Doll and I want to tell you what we found."

The Dolls gathered in the kitchen, Baby Betsy propped against the icebox, her head resting just below the top.

"It was so exciting!" Annabelle began.

"Do you know where Auntie Sarah is?" asked Nanny.

"Well, no. We don't," Uncle Doll replied grimly.

"But we found something fantastic," said Annabelle. "We found another family of dollhouse dolls."

"The Funcrafts," added Bobby. "They're going to be Nora's dolls."

"They're in a big box now with their dream house. There's a mother and a father, a boy for Bobby, a girl for me, and a baby for Baby Betsy."

"And a cat," said Bobby. "Kitty Funcraft."

"But it's not alive," said Uncle Doll quickly.

"The Funcrafts are a birthday present for Nora," Annabelle went on. "I promised them that as soon as they've been unpacked and set up in her room, we'll visit them."

"All of us?" asked Nanny. "My stars, I don't believe I've been out of this house in years."

"It will be okay," said Annabelle kindly.

"It *would* be nice to meet some other dolls," said Papa. "If we can do it safely."

"We must be sure to bring them a housewarming gift," said Mama thoughtfully. "I wonder what they'll need in their new home."

"We can't take them something that belongs here

in our house," Papa reminded her. "Nora will get in trouble."

"Maybe we can make something," said Annabelle. "We'll do it secretly at night."

And so the long, long hours—the hours of waiting for Nora's birthday to arrive, for her gifts to be given to her, for the dream house to be unpacked and set up in her room—were filled by secret meetings about what to make for the Funcrafts. Finally, Nanny suggested using scraps of paper and bits of crayons that the Dolls had squirreled away over the years to make a bouquet of paper flowers for the Funcrafts. Early on the morning after Nora's birthday, the bouquet was completed.

"Now hide everything carefully," said Nanny, surveying the snippets of paper and the shavings of crayons strewn across the kitchen table.

Annabelle and Bobby cleaned up while Mama arranged the flowers and tied their stems with a bit of thread.

"We'll take them to the Funcrafts tonight," said Annabelle.

That evening, just minutes after Kate had

closed her book and turned off her light, Annabelle thought she heard a noise from the doorway. The Captain, she thought. Of all nights for him to decide to prowl. The Dolls would have to wait—

"Yoo-hoo!" called a small voice from below the Dolls' house.

Annabelle lay rigidly in her bed. She knew she shouldn't risk moving about yet.

"Yoo-hoo!" called the voice again.

"Down here!" added another.

"Bobby," Annabelle dared to whisper. "I think the Funcrafts are here."

"Hush! Not another word!" Nanny called softly from her room.

But it was too late. Annabelle could hear the sound of feet scampering up the steps of the stool. "We can't just ignore them," she said.

Cautiously, Annabelle slipped out of her bed. She crossed her room and tiptoed down the stairs to the second floor. "Somebody has to greet them," she said before Mama or Papa could scold her. "They're already on the top step."

"Heavenly days," said Papa.

Mama said nothing.

Annabelle hurried to the first floor and stood at the bottom of the staircase. There, gathered on the top step of the stool, were five dolls. They were unlike any dolls Annabelle had ever seen. One of them stepped forward.

"Hi! I'm Tiffany," she said.

Annabelle looked at the light brown face with dark brown hair topped by a pink bow. The head was poised on a pink-and-blue dress, and stick-thin legs emerged from a pair of wide blue shoes. The doll's arms were as skinny as her legs. And she seemed to be made entirely of plastic. Even her clothes.

"Hi. I'm Annabelle," Annabelle replied.

She peered behind Tiffany. She saw three more dolls, all made of plastic. One was carrying a baby, which was just a small pink bundle.

Bobby had crept down the stairs and was now standing beside Annabelle. "I'm Bobby," he said. "Mama and Papa aren't sure we should talk to you yet. Kate just went to sleep, and—"

"It's all right, Bobby," said Papa. He was

tiptoeing bravely down the stairs, followed by Mama, Uncle Doll, and Nanny. He held his hand out toward Mom and Dad Funcraft. "Welcome, welcome," he said.

Annabelle took a better look at Tiffany, and saw that, in fact, everything about her *was* plastic. Plastic, plastic, plastic—down to the pink bow. And Annabelle suspected that the bow snapped on, just as the writing on the box had said.

Annabelle stopped staring and remembered her manners.

"Mama, Papa, Nanny," she began, "these are the Funcrafts."

"And you must be the Dolls," said the man with the red tie. "I'm Dad," he added.

"I'm Mom," said Mom.

"I'm Bailey," said the boy with the red shoes.

"And this is Baby Britney," said Tiffany.

"Who takes care of the baby?" Bobby wanted to know.

"Of Baby Britney? We all do," replied Bailey.

"Don't you have a nanny?"

"No."

"And no auntie or uncle?"

"No."

"Want to see my train?" asked Bobby.

"Okay." Bailey followed Bobby up the stairs.

"Please, come into our parlor," said Mama graciously to the rest of the Funcrafts.

"Thank you," said Dad.

"How quaint," said Mom.

Annabelle took Tiffany by the hand. "Let's go into the kitchen so we can be by ourselves."

Tiffany walked around and around the kitchen, examining everything.

"Where's your microwave?" she asked.

"Microwave?" said Annabelle.

"You know. Where you pretend to cook your food."

"You mean our stove? That's where we cook," said Annabelle, pointing.

"What are those things?"

"That's a potato masher and that's an orange squeezer and that's a whisk."

"Boy, your house is different from ours."

"It's over one hundred years old. Just like us."

"Are you really over a hundred?" asked Tiffany incredulously.

"Yes. Even though Kate decided I'm eight."

"Wow. I guess that's why you look so different, too."

Tiffany took in the lacy sleeves of the dress, the china arms and legs, the china face, the blush on Annabelle's cheeks, and the green paint in her hair.

"Was your hair always green?" she asked.

"No. A long time ago, when Grandma Katherine was six years old, she decided to give me a new hair color. So she

painted my hair green, and then her mother tried to remove it, but she couldn't get it all off."

"It's very punk," said Tiffany. "I like it."

At that moment Annabelle heard a small commotion outside the kitchen. She rushed to the stairway in time to see Mom Funcraft exclaim, "Oh, look.

The Dolls have stairs, too!" Mom ran up to the landing and slid down the banister, landing smartly on the floor between Mama and Papa.

Dad Funcraft smiled proudly. "She's an expert," he said.

Annabelle glanced at her parents. They were peering frantically into Kate's room, searching for signs that she had awakened.

"Generally," said Papa, "we refrain from making much noise for about two more hours. Until we are certain the entire Palmer household is sound asleep."

"Oh, they won't hear us," said Mom. "And if they do, we'll just hide."

Annabelle saw her parents cringe.

Mom and Dad Funcraft gazed around the Dolls' parlor.

"Your furniture is so . . ." Mom started to say.

"So old," Tiffany finished for her. "Mom, the Dolls are more than *one hundred* years old. Right, Annabelle?"

"Yes," said Annabelle.

"Don't you have anything plastic?" asked Tiffany.

Annabelle had never thought about this, but she replied quickly, "Of course we do. Mama, where's the lamp Kate's mother bought for us when she was little?"

"The Lava lamp?" replied Mama. "Oh, it's not here anymore. Mrs. Palmer took it out later. It didn't go with the decor."

"I think a Lava lamp looks nice anywhere," said Tiffany.

The Funcrafts explored the rest of the house. They tested the keys on the piano. They remarked upon a 1933 edition of *National Geographic* that lay on a table in the parlor. Bailey tried the rocking horse in the nursery, and then leaped from it onto Bobby's bed, while Mom and Dad looked on, smiling. Annabelle was amazed.

Finally, everyone gathered in the kitchen, where the Funcrafts had no end of questions. Tiffany was proud to be able to identify the potato masher, the orange squeezer, and the whisk for her parents.

"Interesting," said Mom.

"Where are your barbecue things?" asked Dad.

"Barbecue?" repeated Nanny. She turned to Mama and Papa, and they shrugged. "I guess we don't have barbecue things."

"What's a barbecue?" Annabelle asked Tiffany.

"It's a grill. A gas grill."

"You turn it on," added Mom, "and it cooks food quickly. With the great taste of the outdoors. Of course, ours doesn't really work. But we have fun pretending."

"A barbecue," said Tiffany, "is also a party—like a picnic—at which you serve the barbecued food."

"Picnic?" said Annabelle. "We don't know what that is either."

"You're kidding. Our dream house came with a picnic basket. It's one of the basic items."

"But if you want picnic foods for the basket you have to order separately," said Dad.

"My goodness" was all Mama Doll could say.

Mom Funcraft whispered something to Dad Funcraft and then to Bailey and Tiffany, who grinned. Then she said to the Dolls, "Would you like to come over to our house for a barbecue one night? We could have a getting-to-know-you party."

Annabelle looked hopefully at Mama, who was looking at Papa. She knew her mother was having second thoughts about visiting the Funcrafts, now that she had met them. "Well," said Mama finally, "all right."

Yes! thought Annabelle.

"How about tomorrow night?"

"Tomorrow night? Oh, I don't think . . ."

"Please come," said Mom. "We'll have a wonderful party. Don't you want to see our house, Mrs. Doll?"

"We have a computer and a VCR," added Dad.

"Also a patio," said Bailey. "That's where we'll have the barbecue."

"Well . . ." said Mama helplessly.

"Oh, please, Mama," said Annabelle. "We made them the . . . you know what. Please?"

"Very well," Mama said to Mom Funcraft. "Thank you."

"Fantastic!" exclaimed Mom. "We'll see you tomorrow night."

The Funcrafts turned to leave.

"See you!" Tiffany called as she and her family slid down the steps of the stool.

" 'Bye," replied Annabelle. She looked at her parents. They were staring at each other in disbelief.

"To think," said Nanny, "that we've gone all these years without a single neighbor, and then we end up with such unusual ones."

"I suppose we must give them a chance," said Mama cautiously.

"But they're so raucous," said Papa.

"Still, they *are* our neighbors," said Mama.

"True," said Uncle Doll.

"And we must be neighborly."

"They don't seem like *bad* people," added Nanny.

"No," agreed Papa. "Just different."

"There's nothing wrong with being different," said Mama.

"I like them," declared Annabelle. "I can't wait for tomorrow night."

CHAPTER SIX

Annabelle Downstairs

NNABELLE spent a good portion of the next day planning exactly how she would present the bouquet of paper flowers to the Funcrafts that night. Although she knew she ought to give them to Mom Funcraft, she wanted badly to give them to Tiffany. She planned to hold them behind her back as she and her family entered Nora's room. Then, just as she stepped through the front door of the dream house, she would pull the bouquet out, thrust it toward Tiffany, and say grandly, "A floral bouquet for your new home. This is a housewarming gesture from my family to yours. We hope you like it. We made it ourselves."

Annabelle was busily memorizing her speech that afternoon when she heard a commotion in the hallway outside Kate's room. A moment later, Nora burst through the doorway carrying the bucket of farm animals.

Not Rancher Family again! Annabelle thought, feeling panicky, but all she could do was stand, disgusted, in the parlor where she had been left that morning.

From her spot near the sofa, Annabelle had a good view of Nora and the bucket. She watched, her stomach sinking, as Nora dumped the bucket on Kate's floor and reached into the pile of animals and toys. Then, hands full, Nora ran to the Dolls' house, climbed the stool, and emptied her hands in the parlor. To Annabelle's great surprise, she found herself face-to-face with Tiffany.

Annabelle wanted to shout. She wanted to grab Tiffany and tell her what Rancher Family was. At the very least she wanted to grin. But she didn't move so much as an eyebrow, and neither did Tiffany.

"Hum, hum, de-hum," murmured Nora. She dumped another handful of toys in the parlor. Annabelle was now surrounded by Tiffany, Mom Funcraft, Bailey, a goose, two hens, two cows, a horse, and four pigs.

Nora set the animals on one side of the room. She moved Annabelle, Tiffany, Mom, and Bailey to the other side.

"The all-new Rancher Family," said Nora. "Here, you old dollies. Look at my new dollies." Nora picked up Annabelle in one hand and Tiffany in the other. She held them about two inches apart. "You be nice to my new dollies, all you old dollies," she went on. "They have never played Rancher Family before, so you have to help them. Annabelle, you go first. You will show the horse riding."

Nora dropped Tiffany to the parlor floor, and Annabelle winced. She had been dropped like that herself, and had the chips and cracks to show for it. But Tiffany didn't crack when she landed. She seemed to bounce a little. And—had Tiffany smiled slightly?

Nora pulled Annabelle's skirt up and stuck her legs over the back of the horse. "Ride 'em, cowboy!" she cried, and she galloped Annabelle through the house.

"Okay, your turn, new dolly," she said as she returned Annabelle and the horse to the parlor. She pulled Annabelle off, tossed her on the couch, and stuck Tiffany on the horse instead. Then she sat Bailey and Mom Funcraft on the cows. "Time for the roundup! Gallop, gallop, gallop."

Nora ran the Funcrafts through the house so fast that Mom fell off the cow and landed on the sofa, and Bailey toppled forward and fell over the cow's head and into the kitchen sink.

Oh. Oh, no, thought Annabelle. What a horrible experience for the Funcrafts. I hope Tiffany won't be mad at me. I should have warned her about Rancher Family. I should have—

Annabelle's thoughts were cut short when Nora left the room for a minute and Bailey leaped up in the sink, shouting, "Awesome!"

while Mom Funcraft stood on the couch and bounced on the cushions.

Annabelle stared at them, openmouthed.

"For heaven's sake, get *down*, both of you!" hissed Papa Doll. "Do you want Nora to—"

Nora sailed back into the room then, carrying a bottle of baby powder. Bailey collapsed in the sink, and Mom draped herself over the couch cushions.

Annabelle could not believe what she had just seen. The Funcrafts were enjoying themselves.

"Look, you new dollies," said Nora. "I brought the rest of your family." Sure enough, Nora was also clutching Dad Funcraft and Baby Britney. She tossed them in the parlor, then twisted the cap on the powder. "Time for the snowstorm!" she said.

"Nora!" exclaimed a voice from the doorway.

Nora jumped, and turned around guiltily.

The voice belonged to Kate. "What are you doing?" she said to Nora.

"Playing with . . ." Nora's voice trailed off.

Annabelle watched as Kate slowly entered her room. Kate looked in the Dolls' house. She saw the Dolls. She saw the Funcrafts. She saw Nora's revolting plastic animals.

"Nora, you have your own dollhouse now," Kate said, trying her best to be patient. "You have your own dolls. Why are you still playing Rancher Family in my dollhouse?"

"Well, because I wanted my dollies to meet your dollies."

"But, Nora, you know I don't like the animals in the dollhouse."

Thank you, Kate, thought Annabelle.

"Everything doesn't have to be *your* way," cried Nora.

"But we have rules," said Kate.

"I hate rules!"

"Nora." Kate drew in a deep breath. "Please take your dolls and all the animals back to your room. Okay?"

"You are not the boss of me."

Kate ignored this. "Poor Dolls," she said,

reaching into the parlor. "Okay, it's teatime for you." She settled Annabelle back on the couch. Then she scooped up the Funcrafts and began to gather the farm animals for Nora.

Goody, thought Annabelle.

Annabelle was imagining a pleasant, cow-free afternoon when suddenly she felt herself being pulled and squished, snatched from the dollhouse.

"Ha!" cried Nora.

Thump, thump, thump. Annabelle bounced along as Nora ran from Kate's room. Nora's hand covered Annabelle's face. It was dark and Annabelle didn't dare move. Except her eyes. She looked around and realized she could see through a small crack between Nora's fingers. Annabelle watched the hallway wallpaper fly by. The wallpaper ended, and—*bump, bump, bump*—Nora hurried down the stairs.

"Nora!" shouted Kate from the hallway.

Nora didn't stop. She jumped down the

last two steps, and Annabelle thought she rec-
ognized the living room furniture.

"Nora, give Annabelle back!" cried Kate.

"No!"

"Yes!"

"NO!"

The next thing Annabelle knew she was
flying through the air. She landed with a bump
on something soft. Soft and red and woolly. A
sweater, Annabelle guessed. A sweater lying on
the floor? That seemed odd, but she didn't
dare look around or move her head.

"Where's Annabelle?" Kate cried. "Did
you throw her, Nora? She's china. She'll
break!"

At this, Grandma Katherine hurried
into the room. "Nora. Kate. Settle down,"
she said.

"But Nora took—" Kate started to say, at
the same time Nora started to say, "But Kate
won't let me—"

Grandma Katherine held up her hands.
"Hush," she said. "Kate, we will look for
Annabelle later. Nora, come with me and
help me set the table for dinner."

Before long, Annabelle was forgotten.

Sometime later—Annabelle wasn't sure just how long—she heard the Palmers sit down to supper in the dining room. She pulled herself out of the awkward position in which she'd landed and sat up. Yes, she was perched on a sweater. It was old, full of holes, and covered with fur. Cat fur.

Oh, *ew*, thought Annabelle. This must be one of The Captain's beds. He must sleep here when he doesn't sleep in Kate's room.

Annabelle stood up and peered around. She was in the living room, in a corner behind an armchair. She sighed and sat down again. She listened to the voices drifting out of the dining room. Kate was talking about third grade. Nora was talking about princesses. Annabelle lost interest and began to think about an escape. She wondered what Auntie Sarah would have done if she were in Annabelle's situation. Blended, maybe. Blended in with her surroundings as if she belonged wherever she was. But Annabelle wasn't sure she had enough courage to try something so bold.

The Palmers finished their supper. Annabelle sat nervously on The Captain's bed

and waited for Kate to come looking for her. Instead Mr. Palmer announced that it was homework time, and Kate thumped up the stairs.

Annabelle waited. And waited. Any moment now, she thought, Kate would remember that Annabelle was missing and would come looking for her.

But Kate must have forgotten.

One by one, the people in the house went to bed. First Nora, then Kate, then Grandma Katherine. Finally Mr. and Mrs. Palmer turned out the lights and went upstairs. Soon the house was dark and silent.

And Annabelle was still perched on The Captain's bed.

Most nights when Annabelle lay in the dollhouse waiting for the Palmers to fall asleep, she prayed that The Captain had fallen asleep somewhere on the first floor. Tonight she prayed that he was curled up at the foot of Kate's bed.

Annabelle lay quietly for a moment, then began to edge her way into a more comfortable position. Her hand brushed against something cold and hard and vaguely slimy.

Annabelle scrambled to her feet and stumbled backward. One of the cows from Nora's Rancher Family bucket clattered onto the floor next to her. She sat on something soft and furry and nearly let out a shriek. When she got a look at the furry thing in the moonlight shining through the living room window, she nearly shrieked again. It was a mouse. But it wasn't moving. Annabelle dared to lean over and look at it more closely. It was a very realistic-looking toy mouse. Wasn't it? Annabelle hoped so because if it had stood on its hind legs it would have come nearly to her shoulders. She put out her hand and touched it. Yes. It was just a toy. Annabelle let out a deep sigh.

What else was here in The Captain's bed? No longer so afraid, she felt around. There was the cow again, full of bite marks. Apparently The Captain chewed on the Rancher Family toys. Next Annabelle found a plastic chicken with one leg bitten entirely off, and a tiny cloth doll that she remembered Kate making for Nora one rainy day.

Annabelle lay still for a while and listened to the sounds of the quiet house—a creak, a window shade flapping, the dripping of water in the kitchen sink, the hum of the refrigerator. And then she heard a sound that made her china skin feel colder than ever.

It was a loud purr.

That's it, thought Annabelle. I have to move. I *must* get out of here. If Auntie Sarah were here, she wouldn't just sit around waiting to get chewed up. She'd risk moving. And so will I. I am not going to sit on The Captain's bed until he—

Two glowing eyes rounded a nearby couch. That was all Annabelle could see of The Captain. Just his eyes, shining in the dark. The Captain was not more than three feet away.

Annabelle leaped to her feet. She dashed underneath the armchair. She lay in the dark, breathing hard. Now what? What should she do? She could stay there for a while, but by morning she wanted to be at least partially in sight. She wanted someone to see her and return her to the dollhouse. But she did not want The Captain to see her first. And she could not move far from the spot where she had landed when Nora had thrown her.

Foolish acts such as those made humans suspicious and jeopardized all of dollkind (according to Nanny).

Annabelle listened for The Captain. She hoped to hear the *pad, pad, pad*ding that meant he was kneading the old sweater, getting ready to settle down on it. Instead she heard a faint *whoosh*. And a great furry paw stretched under the chair and swiped at Annabelle.

Okay, that does it, thought Annabelle. She wriggled away from The Captain, thinking fast. If I can just escape from him now, I'll move back to where I'm supposed to be before anyone wakes up tomorrow.

Annabelle crawled out from under the couch. She looked around and decided to run to the matching armchair on the other side of the room. The Captain wouldn't even know she'd left. He'd probably spend all night swiping his paw under the wrong chair.

Here goes, thought Annabelle. She took off across the room. And ran directly into someone's foot. Annabelle heard a gasp. She flopped onto the floor and lay on her back so she could look up. She had run into Mrs. Palmer.

Mrs. Palmer, dressed in her robe and slippers, was on her way to the kitchen.

"Annabelle?" she whispered. She bent down.

Annabelle found herself in Doll State.

CHAPTER SEVEN

Doll State

RS. PALMER picked up Annabelle. "I thought I saw you—" she started to say. Then she shook her head. "Silly . . . impossible."

Annabelle, lifeless, hung stiffly from between Mrs. Palmer's fingers.

Mrs. Palmer muttered something else, then set Annabelle on the edge of the coffee table. "The girls should know better," she said. And she continued toward the kitchen. Twice, though, she looked over her shoulder at Annabelle. And she stared at her on her way back to the stairs.

Doll State. Annabelle was in Doll State again. She remembered the last time she'd been in Doll State, and imagined what was going to happen next. In the morning, Mrs. Palmer would have a talk with the girls, then scold Nora and tell her she had nearly tripped over Annabelle in the dark. Think how horrible it would have been if I had stepped on Annabelle, she would say. I could have crushed her. Then Kate would carry Annabelle back to the dollhouse and most likely put her to bed. The Dolls would wait patiently for the Palmers to leave. When the coast was clear, Mama and Papa would call to Annabelle. She wouldn't be able to answer them. And then everyone would know she was in Doll State. Again.

In her mind, Annabelle sighed. She lay on the coffee table and tried to entertain herself by thinking amusing thoughts. But she was too cross. She couldn't think of anything funny. This was the night her family was supposed to visit the Funcrafts. Had they gone without Annabelle? Was she missing the fun?

Annabelle tried thinking about her birthday. It was coming up soon. May 12. A spring birthday. Annabelle thought spring birthdays were the nicest of all. In the Doll family, Annabelle's birthday came first, then Nanny's, then Papa's, then Uncle Doll's, then Baby Betsy's, then Mama's, then Auntie Sarah's, and finally Bobby's. Their birthdays were the dates on which, over a century ago, the old doll maker had completed them, had put the final touches on them and at last said, "There. All done," and let out a small, proud sigh, which had made his white mustache puff out. When he had finished Annabelle he placed her on a wooden shelf in his workshop in London, next to several other completed dolls. That evening, after he left his workshop, the doll nearest to Annabelle had nudged her.

"It's time to take the oath," she had said.

"What?" Annabelle had not felt quite awake yet. She was still in the half-sleep state in which she'd found herself when the doll maker finished her that afternoon. Before that, she had not been conscious at all.

"You should take the oath now," the other doll said. "The Doll Code of Honor. You have to take it now while no humans are present. Repeat after me. 'I, Annabelle, an avowed member of the race of dolls . . .' "

"I, Annabelle, an avowed member of the race of dolls," Annabelle repeated sleepily.

" '. . . do hereby promise to protect our secret life . . .' "

". . . do hereby promise to protect our secret life . . ." (Annabelle felt more awake.)

" '. . . by upholding the Doll Code of Honor . . .' "

". . . by upholding the Doll Code of Honor . . ."

" '. . . in accordance with its everlasting law.' "

". . . in accordance with its everlasting law."

"In other words," the doll said, "if you err, if you make a mistake and put the secret life of dolls in danger, you could become an ordinary doll again."

An ordinary doll. Even though she had taken the oath over a hundred years earlier, whenever Annabelle remembered this particular moment of her birthday, she shuddered slightly. It made her think about Permanent Doll State. Perhaps there was some truth to it. But Annabelle rarely dwelled on the possibility.

After Annabelle had taken the oath, the other doll said, "You know, you can take back the oath. You don't *have* to be a living doll.

You can choose to be an ordinary one from the start, but that decision is irreversible. Of course, as an ordinary doll your life would be much easier, but it would be—"

"Boring," Annabelle had finished for her, now fully awake. "Forget it. I want to be a living doll. A doll person. I'm sure it's much more fun."

"Very well," the other doll had replied. And then they had talked about Doll State and many other things. But Annabelle was quite certain that the exact words *Permanent Doll State* had never been mentioned.

Three weeks later, the doll maker had completed Nanny. That evening, it was Annabelle who had given Nanny the oath, something she did not let Nanny forget, even though Nanny, *as a nanny*, was the one who now had to remind Annabelle to live by the Doll Code of Honor.

Annabelle knew she would always be a kid, and Nanny

would always be a grown-up. And if somebody had to be a grown-up, Annabelle was glad she wasn't the one.

Annabelle had celebrated her next birthday in the doll maker's shop. But she celebrated the one after that, and all the others, in the house at 26 Wetherby Lane. And Annabelle always remembered to make a secret wish on her birthday. Often the wish came true, which was nearly as good as getting a present.

Annabelle's thoughts drifted to Auntie Sarah's journal. She considered spiders and the Nature Study Exploration. She imagined Auntie Sarah blending near the radio in the living room. Where else might she have blended? Where had her adventures taken her? Had Auntie Sarah ever left the Palmers' house? Had she been . . . Outdoors? Annabelle had not been Outdoors since the day the shipping carton had been delivered to the Coxes' doorstep in 1898. But she thought about the Outdoors often. It was a huge world. It was far bigger than the Dolls' house. It was bigger than Kate's room. It was even bigger than the Palmers' entire house. It was enormous. Annabelle didn't know any doll who had been Outdoors by herself. But she wondered about Auntie Sarah. And she had a feeling the grown-up dolls wondered about her too. She was sure, in fact, that there was something the grown-ups were not telling her about Auntie Sarah and her disappearance. What was it? Were they afraid Auntie Sarah had gone Outdoors? If she had, chances were she would never return or be found. Not after all this time. Were they afraid Auntie Sarah was in Permanent Doll State somewhere? Were they afraid she had been damaged or broken beyond repair?

All those things were scary, but, thought Annabelle, she would much rather know the truth than go on wondering. Mama had said that because they were dolls and could not violate the Doll Code of Honor they had not gone looking for Auntie Sarah. Annabelle had recently decided that she no longer believed this. In fact, a horrible thought occurred to Annabelle as she lay motionless through the long night. The grown-up dolls, she now understood, were afraid to look for Auntie Sarah. *Afraid.* And because of their fear, they were willing to give up on her, on Annabelle's beloved auntie. Not fair, thought Annabelle. Not *right*.

As soon as I can, Annabelle decided as the living room began to grow faintly dusky in the early morning light, I am going to search for Auntie Sarah again. I am going to find her. I will do whatever it takes. Maybe Tiffany can help me. We will read every single word of Auntie Sarah's journal. We might find a clue. We will search every inch of the Palmers' house, even if it takes years. We will search Outdoors if we have to. I don't think Tiffany would be afraid to do any of those things.

Annabelle tried to shift to a more comfortable position on the coffee table, but she couldn't budge. Doll State was so annoying. She simply lay there and waited. And waited. And waited some more.

At long last, morning came, and things happened pretty much the way Annabelle had imagined they would. The next evening, when twenty-four hours had passed and Annabelle was no longer in Doll State, she told her family what had happened. Nanny scolded her, Mama hugged her but gave her a small talking-to, Papa patted her head and told her to try and be more careful, then gave her a small talking-to of his own, and Uncle Doll said, "Tsk. Such a risk." But he whispered to her, "Did you see anything interesting while you were down there?" And Annabelle smiled at him and shook her head.

CHAPTER EIGHT

SELMP

Y THE TIME Annabelle emerged from Doll State, Kate had been asleep for several hours. Annabelle was relieved to learn that her family had not visited the Funcrafts, so she hadn't missed out on the adventure. However, she had other things on her mind. She was determined to continue searching for Auntie Sarah.

Where should I begin? wondered Annabelle. She decided to tackle the secret journal again. But she hadn't completed even one page when she heard a small commotion outside her house. She ran to the nursery window, pleased that, because of Annabelle's disappearance and Kate's annoyance with Nora, the front of the dollhouse had been closed for the night.

"Yoo-hoo!" called a small voice.

"It's us!" called another.

Annabelle leaned as far out her window as she dared, and below her she saw Tiffany and Bailey scrambling up the step stool.

Oh, spectacular! thought Annabelle. "Hello!" she called.

"Annabelle! Oh, my stars!" Nanny caught Annabelle by the bow on her dress and pulled her back into the nursery. "Do you want to fall out the window? For heaven's sake, you were just in Doll State."

"But Tiffany and Bailey are here," Annabelle replied. "And we missed our visit with them last night." She dashed out of the nursery and down the stairs, and threw open the Dolls' front door just as Tiffany, puffing, reached the top step. Bailey was right behind her.

"Hi!" cried Tiffany.

"Hi," replied Annabelle. "We didn't get to go to your house last night. I'm really sorry."

"That's okay. Hey, do you think you could come over right now?"

"I doubt it. Mama and Papa like to be prepared for things."

"But they were prepared to visit us last night. Aren't they still prepared tonight?"

"I don't know," said Annabelle. "They're hard to explain. Besides, they're a little cross with me right now."

Tiffany brightened. "I heard you were in Doll State," she said admiringly.

"Yes. I've been in it lots of times. How about you?"

"None. I haven't had much of a chance," replied Tiffany. "Two weeks ago we were still in the factory in Cleveland."

"Hey," said Annabelle, suddenly curious, "who gave you the oath?" When Tiffany hesitated, she added, "You did take the oath, didn't you?"

"Oh, yes. It's just that I don't know the name of the doll who gave it to us."

"To more than one of you?" asked Annabelle. "You didn't take it by yourself?"

"Well, no. We were in the factory. All the dolls took it at once. There were hundreds of us. I guess some living doll who hadn't left the factory yet gave it to us."

"Girls. Bailey. Come inside, please," said Mama from behind Annabelle. "Quickly. You don't want to wake Kate."

Tiffany and Bailey hurried inside, and Bailey ran off with Bobby, who had followed Annabelle down the stairs.

Annabelle took Tiffany by the hand. "Come to the nursery with me," she whispered. "I have something to show you and something to tell you."

Upstairs, Annabelle was disappointed to discover Bobby and Bailey already in the nursery. "Bobby," she said, "why don't you and Bailey go . . ." Annabelle paused, unable to think where to send them.

"Go slide down the banister," said Tiffany brightly.

"Oh, good idea," said Annabelle, and the boys left the room.

"What do you want to show me?" whispered Tiffany excitedly.

"This," said Annabelle proudly. With a flourish she whisked Auntie Sarah's journal out from under the covers of her bed.

"What's that?"

"Remember my auntie Sarah? The one we were looking for the night we discovered you in your box?"

"Yes," said Tiffany.

"Well, not long ago I found her personal, private journal. It was hidden on a bookshelf. Nobody knew she kept it. I'm sure of it. And nobody knows about the journal now but me. I haven't told a soul. Except you. Auntie Sarah was keeping it the year she disappeared. I think a clue to her disappearance might be in it."

Tiffany drew in her breath. "Are we going to look for clues?" she asked.

"Yes. Just like Nancy Drew."

"Who's Nancy Drew?"

Annabelle told Tiffany about the mysteries Kate was reading.

"You mean we are going to be detectives like Nancy and her friends?"

Annabelle nodded. "I bet all the clues we need are right here in the journal. And when we've discovered them and we think we know where Auntie Sarah is, we will go find her."

"By ourselves?"

"Probably. The grown-ups will never do it. At least not the ones in my family. Well, maybe Uncle Doll, but I don't think so. You're not afraid to go exploring, are you?"

"Me? No, I'm not afraid of anything."

"I didn't think so."

"Tell me about your auntie," said Tiffany.

"Well." Annabelle paused thoughtfully. "She was very brave. And very adventurous. I think she got bored just staying in our house all day long. Day in, day out, nothing changing." Annabelle leaned closer to Tiffany. "You know, I'm a lot like her. I get *so bored* sometimes. I want to do things. I want to try things. I want to go places and see things. But we are stuck here because of the Doll Code of Honor. I don't want to put my family in danger. But I hate having to hold still, and be quiet, and pretend I'm not alive. Do you know what Auntie Sarah used to do?" Tiffany shook her head. "She used to go *blending*."

"Blending? What's that?"

"She would leave our house and go to a room in the Palmers' house and just blend in to the scenery somewhere. You know, make it look as if a human had left her there, even though no one had, of course. But she looked so natural that nobody paid her any attention."

"Oh, that sounds dangerous," said Tiffany.

"Well, it is. If you blend carelessly you could probably end up in Doll State. And I'm pretty sure that blending only tricks the grown-ups. I mean, Kate would always know where she had left a doll."

Tiffany let out a slow whistle. "I can't believe your auntie did that."

"She must have been very good at it," Annabelle said proudly. "I never heard of it until I started reading her journal, so I think she invented it herself. Of course, blending must have scared Mama and Papa and Uncle Doll and Nanny to death. And now that she's gone, I think they fear that the worst has happened."

"You mean . . . Permanent Doll State?"

Annabelle nodded. Then she said, "When Auntie Sarah went blending she could listen to the Palmers, or to the radio. She learned about all sorts of things. That must have been how she was able to tell me about the news and famous people. And adventurous women. Oh, it was wonderful."

"How exciting," said Tiffany. "I wish I had an auntie. One exactly like Auntie Sarah."

"Well, if we could just find Auntie Sarah, I'm sure she would agree to be your auntie as well as mine. She could be your honorary auntie."

"Oh, we've *got* to find her," said Tiffany. "We have to start being detectives right away."

"The first thing to do is finish reading her journal," Annabelle said. "It's hard because, well, look at her handwriting."

Tiffany peered into the book, which lay open on Annabelle's lap. She leaned closer and closer. "Boy, that *is* hard to read. It's all squiggly and crawly and faded."

"I know. But this is where we have to start."

"No, wait! I know what we have to do first."

"What?" asked Annabelle.

"We have to form a society."

"We do?"

"Yes. If we're going to be good explorers, we must belong to an official society."

"All right."

"We'll call ourselves . . ." Tiffany frowned. "We'll call ourselves the Society for Exploration and the Location of Missing Persons."

"That's an awfully long name."

"We'll use the abbreviation. SELMP."

"SELMP? That's a funny word."

"It doesn't matter. We know what it means."

"Okay," said Annabelle.

"And we should meet regularly. Once a week."

"How about twice a week? I mean, if we can."

"Okay, twice a week."

"Oh!" said Annabelle. "I have an idea. We should start every meeting with a secret reading of the journal."

"Yes. We'll see if it gives us any more clues. Then we'll review all our clues."

"And when we think we know where Auntie Sarah is," said Annabelle, "we'll plan an exploration to find her."

"Perfect. That is just what SELMP should be doing."

Annabelle grinned at her new friend. She felt so happy that she didn't even mind (much) when Papa announced that it was time for Tiffany and Bailey to head back to their house.

CHAPTER NINE

Exploring

AS TIFFANY was leaving that night, Annabelle whispered to her, "Let's try to have a SELMP meeting tomorrow night. Maybe if we try to have a meeting *every* night we actually will be able to meet twice a week."

"I promise I'll try to come over every single night," replied Tiffany, who understood that Mom and Dad Funcraft would most likely let her out whenever she asked, while Mama and Papa Doll would rarely let Annabelle out.

But Tiffany didn't show up the next night

and Annabelle knew why. Nora had caught a cold and couldn't sleep. Someone was up with her nearly all night.

The next night, however, Tiffany arrived on the Dolls' doorstep just minutes after Kate had gone to bed.

"You're taking quite a risk," said Papa, looking at the clock as Annabelle let Tiffany inside.

"Nora's already asleep," Tiffany pointed out. "Besides, I was careful."

Annabelle whisked Tiffany upstairs. "Did you see The Captain?" she asked her when they were settled on Annabelle's bed.

"Nope. Not a hair. Anyway, I don't think we have to be so nervous about him. I met a doll in the factory who knew of another doll, and that doll had heard of some dolls in western Canada who trained the cat in their house not to bother them. Trained him like a big horse."

Annabelle's eyes widened. "Do you think we could train The Captain?"

"Sure. Only let's not do it right away. Let's worry about finding Auntie Sarah first. Then we can worry about The Captain."

"All right." Annabelle reached for the secret journal.

"Oh," said Tiffany. "Let's not read the journal tonight. Let's just plan an exploration."

"But how will we know where to search if we don't look for Auntie Sarah's clues in the journal first?"

"I don't know. We'll just go out and look."

"I did that already," replied Annabelle. "That's what Bobby and Uncle Doll and I were doing when we found you instead. I don't know where to look. This is a huge house. Auntie Sarah could be anywhere. She could even be . . . Outside."

"Outside?" Tiffany looked amazed. "Really?"

"Yes. So I thought that the next time we went looking we should know what we're doing."

"But just reading the journal is going to be . . . Well, it won't be as much fun as actually searching."

"I know." Annabelle felt frustrated and wasn't quite sure what to do about it. "Well, we did say that we would start each meeting with a reading of the journal. We said that, didn't we?"

"Yes," admitted Tiffany.

"So let's have the reading." Annabelle opened to the first page of the journal. "I think we should start at the beginning and read all the way through. Not tonight," she added hurriedly. "But eventually. If we read every word we're bound to find clues."

"Okay, but just the first page tonight," said Tiffany.

Even though Annabelle had already read the first page of Auntie Sarah's journal she now read it again to Tiffany.

"Hmm. Interesting," said Tiffany, in a tone that let Annabelle know she didn't find the journal interesting at all.

"We should keep reading," said Annabelle. "All the interesting parts come later."

"But that's enough for now. All right, let's plan our exploration. I think we should go as soon as possible. Tomorrow night if we can. Um, Annabelle, do you think your parents are going to let you go on an exploration with me?"

"Well . . . yes. After all, they already let me go out once, and nothing happened. Nothing dangerous, I mean. And if I tell them that we are really, really, really going to find Auntie Sarah then at least Uncle Doll will want me to go."

"Hmm. Interesting," said Tiffany again, but in an entirely different tone.

Annabelle stared at her for a moment, not certain what Tiffany was thinking. Finally she said, "We should try to leave pretty late at night. Mama and Papa won't let me out unless they are sure all the Palmers are asleep."

"I'll come over tomorrow night as soon as I can," said Tiffany. "Then we'll just wait until your parents say we can leave. Now, where did you and Bobby and your uncle look for Auntie Sarah the night you found us?"

"Just on this floor."

"Then I think we should look downstairs on our exploration."

"It will take a long time to go down the stairs, but all right," replied Annabelle.

That night, as Tiffany was leaving, she whispered to Annabelle, "I'll be back tomorrow night. Talk to your parents before then."

Annabelle did so. She talked to them as soon as the Palmers left the next morning. "I promise we won't be gone long," she said.

"Oh, Annabelle," said Mama. "I can't let you go. Especially without a grown-up."

"But we're going to find Auntie Sarah. We really are. Maybe not tonight, but we *will* find her. Anyway, Tiffany is kind of like a grown-up."

Papa cleared his throat.

Nanny muttered something Annabelle couldn't understand.

But Uncle Doll said, "I don't think it's a bad idea. You'll be careful, won't you, Annabelle?"

"Of course."

Annabelle heard more throat clearing and muttering. And she saw a lot of long looks exchanged between Uncle Doll and the other grown-ups. Then Mama said, "You must promise to stay out no longer than two hours."

"You mean I can go?" squealed Annabelle. "Oh, thank you, Mama!"

That night, Kate was restless and couldn't fall asleep. So Grandma Katherine sat beside her, and by the light from Kate's little table lamp read to her from *Stuart Little*, a book Annabelle liked quite a lot. Grandma Katherine read one chapter, but Kate was not sleepy yet. She began another. Halfway through it, Annabelle, who had been left standing in the kitchen and had a good view of Kate's room, noticed a small movement at Kate's doorway. She looked closely and saw that the shape at the door was Tiffany's. Annabelle nearly gasped. She wondered whether Mama or Papa or Uncle Doll or Nanny had noticed, too, but she couldn't turn her head to look at them. All she could think to do was close her eyes and hope fervently that Tiffany would disappear. So she closed them and hoped. When she opened them again she saw Tiffany scooting under Kate's desk, and then under her bed.

There were so many things wrong with what Tiffany was doing at that moment that Annabelle could barely count them. Tiffany risked being seen by Kate or Grandma Katherine. She risked running into The Captain. She risked Doll State. She risked Permanent Doll State.

Annabelle's head was spinning.

At long last, Kate grew drowsy and fell

asleep, and Grandma Katherine closed the book and turned off the light. She tiptoed out of Kate's room. In a flash, Tiffany sprinted across the room and scaled the steps of the stool. Annabelle stole a glance at Mama and Papa. They were shaking their heads.

Annabelle ran to the edge of the dollhouse. "You're here too soon!" she said in a loud whisper.

"Did you see what I was doing?" interrupted Tiffany.

"I—" Annabelle began to say.

"I was blend—"

"Shhh!" Annabelle cut her off. "We aren't supposed to know about that, and anyway that was *not* proper blending." Annabelle was so nervous about Mama and Papa and the exploration that she was shaking a little. "Tiffany, we are not going to be allowed to go," she said. "Mama and Papa did say I could search for Auntie Sarah, but I think they meant sometime in the future. Tonight they're all nervous because they've seen The Captain prowling around."

But Annabelle was allowed to go after all, and it was Uncle Doll who saved the day.

When Mama and Papa told Annabelle they thought it was too dangerous for her to go searching for Auntie Sarah after all, Uncle Doll simply said, quietly but very firmly, "I am not going to let this happen again."

Mama and Papa fell silent.

Two hours later, Annabelle and Tiffany were climbing down the steps of the stool. They didn't say a word until they reached the hallway outside.

"I wish you could come see my house," Tiffany whispered.

"So do I," replied Annabelle. "But we don't have much time tonight. Only two hours before I have to be back home. We had better start searching right away. I'll get to see your house another time." She almost added, "And maybe Auntie Sarah will be with me." Then she thought better of it. She didn't want to jinx the exploration.

"All right. Where are the stairs?" asked Tiffany.

"This way." Annabelle showed Tiffany to the top of the flight of stairs that led to the living room below. Tiffany looked down. "Wow. It is a long way. . . . Okay. Let's get started."

Fifteen minutes later Annabelle and Tiffany sat puffing on the living room rug. Annabelle looked up at the grandfather clock. "Come on," she said. "Let's look here in the living room first. I've been wondering if Auntie Sarah had an accident while she was blending. And I think she did most of her blending here, because this is where the Palmers used to spend their evenings. The big radio was in this room."

"You know what?" said Tiffany. "If Auntie Sarah fell off of a table or something, she could have gone down one of the heating vents. Let's call down all the vents."

So Annabelle and Tiffany called softly down the vents. Then they looked under the couches and armchairs.

"There's The Captain's bed," Annabelle said to

Tiffany, pointing to the old sweater. "He's not in it. I wonder where he is."

Annabelle didn't see him that night, though.

And she and Tiffany didn't find Auntie Sarah.

Finally, Annabelle, glancing again at the grandfather clock, said, "We have to be back in fifteen minutes, Tiffany. We'll just make it on time."

But Annabelle had forgotten that it would take a lot longer to climb up the stairs than it had taken to scramble down them. By the time she and Tiffany arrived, puffing, at the doorway to Kate's room, they were nearly half an hour late.

"This is not good," Annabelle whispered. "Mama and Papa are going to be angry."

"Do you want me to come with you?" asked Tiffany, glancing toward the Dolls' house.

"No. Thank you. That's okay. I had better go by myself. Come over again tomorrow night, though."

"All right. See you." Tiffany hurried down the hall to Nora's room.

And Annabelle returned to her house.

When at last she scaled the top step of the stool, she found herself facing Mama and Papa Doll. They were standing in the parlor with their arms folded across their chests, waiting for her.

Oops, thought Annabelle.

CHAPTER TEN

Uncle Doll Moves Out

NNABELLE, we were worried about you," said Mama.

"Very worried," said Papa.

"I know, I know. I'm sorry. I knew you'd be worried. I forgot how long it would take us to climb back up the stairs."

"Annabelle, we cannot continue to let you leave the house if you are not going to be responsible about it," said Papa.

"I was trying to be responsible. I really was," said Annabelle. "I told Tiffany fifteen minutes ahead of time that we had to stop looking. But the stairs—"

Annabelle was interrupted by Uncle Doll. "Did you see any sign of Auntie Sarah?" he asked.

Papa Doll looked as though he were going to say something, but he kept his mouth closed.

"No," replied Annabelle. "Not a sign. We called down the heating vents, in case she had fallen down one, and we searched the rest of the living room. We thought we'd look in the kitchen the next time we go out." She glanced at Mama and Papa. "I can go again, can't I?" she said, even though she knew this probably wasn't the best time to ask such a question.

Mama clasped her hands together. "I don't know, Annabelle," she said. "I—" She glanced at Papa. "We . . . can't make that promise."

Annabelle stood very still. "Please," she said at last. "This is important to me."

"And *you* are important to *us*," said Papa.

"When you are late," Mama continued slowly, "we sit here and worry about you. Worry that, just like Auntie Sarah, you won't come home at all."

"But—" said Annabelle. She glanced at

Uncle Doll. "I—" Uncle Doll sat on the sofa. He put his head in his hands. Nanny sat next to him. Annabelle looked at them. She looked at Mama and Papa standing stiffly in the doorway. "What," said Annabelle quietly, "really happened to Auntie Sarah? You know, don't you? All you grown-ups. You know the truth. And you won't tell me."

"No," said Mama. "That isn't so, Annabelle. We don't know what happened to her."

"But you know something," said Annabelle. "And you won't tell me what it is."

"It isn't that so much," Papa Doll began. "It's that we had a disagreement—"

"An argument," interrupted Uncle Doll.

"All right, an argument," said Papa. "An argument about what we did after Auntie Sarah disappeared."

"An argument about what we *didn't* do," muttered Uncle Doll.

"I don't understand," said Annabelle.

Mama Doll sighed. "Your uncle felt we

should have made more of an effort to find her," she said.

"We should have made *any* effort," said Uncle Doll. "We didn't do a thing."

"We *couldn't*," spoke up Nanny. "We would have put ourselves in danger. We would have jeopardized—"

"We could have figured out how to search for her," said Uncle Doll. "But we never went looking. Not once."

"How could we have?" asked Mama.

"Well, *I* just looked for her," said Annabelle.

"And we feel that you put yourself in danger," said Papa.

"Then why did you let me go?"

Mama and Papa looked pointedly at Uncle Doll.

"Because it's time we laid aside our fears and let common sense take over," said Uncle Doll.

"Running around the Palmers' house in the middle of the night and risking being seen is not common sense," said Mama.

Annabelle was looking from Mama to Papa to Nanny to Uncle Doll. She had never heard the grown-ups fight before. And now they were fighting and Annabelle was the cause of it.

Papa walked across the room and stood directly in front of Uncle Doll. "Just what, exactly, do you think we should have done forty-five years ago when Auntie Sarah didn't come back?"

"I think we should have looked for her until we found her. We should have gone out in teams. We should have scoured the house, searched it inch by inch, from top to bottom."

"That," said Mama between clenched teeth, "violates the code."

"If it violates the code, how did Sarah manage to leave the house on more than one occasion and keep coming back here?"

Annabelle drew in her breath. She wondered how often her aunt had left.

Before Annabelle could say anything, Mama Doll snapped, "She went one step too far and *didn't* come back. She *did* violate the code. And that is what is going to happen to Annabelle if she keeps leaving the house."

"But maybe," said Annabelle, "Auntie

Sarah is missing because of something that has nothing to do with the code. Maybe she's just stuck somewhere."

"And she's been waiting all these years for her family to come and find her," Uncle Doll added pointedly.

Annabelle thought then of the question she had asked her parents that they hadn't answered. "If I were missing," she began, "if I went out and didn't come back for days, wouldn't you come looking for me? Or would you just sit in the house and talk about me?"

"Annabelle, don't be insolent," said Nanny.

"But," said Annabelle, "I want to know."

"Well?" said Uncle Doll, looking at Mama and Papa and Nanny. "What are you going to tell her? That you'd worry your heads off—while you sat around the piano in the middle of the night singing 'Respect'?"

"Don't put words in our mouths," replied Papa.

"You really don't care what I think, do you?" said Uncle Doll. "Just because I have a different opinion about this, because I don't agree with the three of you . . . then you're right and I'm wrong. Well, guess what. I'm tired of that." Uncle Doll paused. "And guess what else. I'm moving out."

"You're what?" exclaimed Mama.

"I'm moving out."

Annabelle heard a slight noise behind her and realized that Bobby, who had been playing in the nursery, was now standing at the bottom of the stairs, watching and listening. He ran to Uncle Doll. "You can't move out!" he cried. "Where would you go?"

And Nanny said, "Oh, now don't be silly."

"I'm not being silly," said Uncle Doll. "This is serious to me."

"This is all *my* fault," said Annabelle with a small moan.

"No, it isn't," Uncle Doll replied. "I'm proud of you, Annabelle. You are the only one of all of us with true integrity."

Annabelle frowned. True integrity? She tucked the words away in her head. She would discuss them with Tiffany later.

Uncle Doll ran up the stairs to his room.

A few minutes later he returned with several items tossed in a handkerchief, which he tied to a matchstick and placed over his shoulder. "Farewell," he said gravely, as he threw the pack down the top step of the stool and began to climb after it.

"But where are you going?" asked Annabelle.

"To . . ." Uncle Doll looked around. "To . . . the camper," he said with finality.

Annabelle watched as Uncle Doll slid down the steps, landed on the floor of Kate's room, and hurried to the pink Barbie camper under the window. After a few minutes, she followed him. When she reached the camper, she pulled open the door. Uncle Doll was reclining on an uncomfortable looking cot, which Annabelle was fairly certain had not been part of the camper originally. Kate's fourth Barbie, this one with long chestnut-colored hair, sat on the floor next to him, smiling quizzically.

Annabelle pointed to the Barbie. "Permanent Doll State?" she asked Uncle Doll.

"No. Didn't take the oath. Barbies never do."

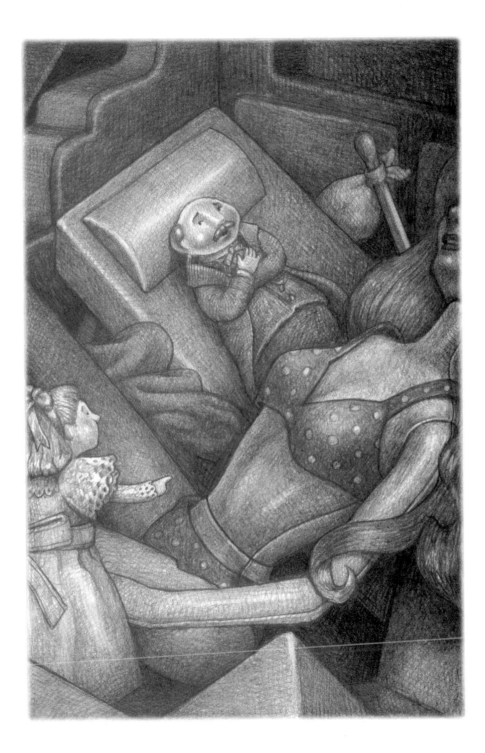

"Uncle Doll, please come home. I don't want you to move out."

"I need some time to think."

"Well, what are you going to do in the morning? You can't let Kate find you in here with your pack. That would definitely violate the code."

"I know. I'll have to go back to the house before Kate wakes up. But during the day when the Palmers are out, and at night when Kate's asleep, this is going to be my home."

"For how long?"

"I don't know. Until your parents and I sort some things out." Annabelle didn't know what to say. "I know you don't understand, Annabelle," Uncle Doll went on. "This is just the way things have to be for a while."

"All right. I guess you want to be alone now."

Uncle Doll nodded, so Annabelle left him and returned to the dollhouse. She went directly to her room and lay on her bed read-ing Auntie Sarah's diary until it was time for Kate to wake up.

All the next day, while Kate was at school and Uncle Doll was thinking in Barbie's camper, Annabelle read the diary. No one disturbed her. She concentrated harder than ever, and by that night, when Kate was asleep and Annabelle was able to open the journal again, she was more than halfway through it. She had read another ten pages when Tiffany appeared in the nursery.

"Oh!" said Annabelle, startled.

"Sorry," said Tiffany. "I didn't mean to scare you."

"That's okay. I was just reading the journal. I've been reading it forever. Everyone's leaving me alone."

"Are you being punished?"

Annabelle shook her head. "No. Not really. But I have a lot to tell you."

Tiffany sat on the end of the bed, tucking her feet under her. Annabelle began to relate the events of the previous night. When she reached the part about Uncle Doll moving out, Tiffany ran to the edge of the nursery and looked across Kate's room at the camper. "Is that where he's living?" she asked.

"Part-time," replied Annabelle.

"That's called a Barbie camper?"

"Yes."

"What's a Barbie?"

"A doll. They probably don't make them in Marwin Ink Factory, though. Kate has about seven Barbies. Nora has three."

"And that's Barbie's dollhouse?"

"Well, sort of."

Tiffany returned to the bed and sat down again. She looked serious. "I can't imagine how I would feel if Mom or Dad moved out of our house."

"The worst thing," said Annabelle, "is that it's all my fault."

"But your uncle said you have true integrity."

"What do you think that means?"

"I'm not sure exactly, but I know it's a good thing. Like, you're very clear about what you believe in, and you stand up for yourself. Or something. Anyway, he certainly doesn't seem mad at you. He seems proud." Annabelle nodded. "But about Auntie Sarah . . . I wonder what happened when she disappeared."

"Well, of course Uncle Doll is mad because Mama and Papa and Nanny refused to look for her," said Annabelle. "But I have a feeling there's something more. I keep trying to remember. I've been reading her journal all day for clues. You know what, Tiffany? We just *have* to find Auntie Sarah. I have a feeling that's the only way the grown-ups are going to stop being mad at one another. I made them get mad, and now I have to make them apologize. But I don't think that's going to happen without Auntie Sarah."

"Are you *certain* she's in the house somewhere, Annabelle?"

"Not positive. But I *think* she is. And that she's okay. I just have a feeling about it."

Tiffany moved closer to Annabelle and peered at the journal. "Okay," she said. "Let's keep reading. We have a lot of work to do."

CHAPTER ELEVEN

The Attic

ANNABELLE opened Auntie Sarah's journal and pointed to a page in it. "I've read this much," she said to Tiffany.

"That's a lot. Tell me what's happening now."

"Well, this journal started early in nineteen fifty-five. I don't know whether Auntie Sarah kept other journals. I think maybe not."

"Why don't you think so?" asked Tiffany.

"Because at the beginning of this one she wrote about regular things—you know, what she and our family did every day, what we did at night, what Katherine and her husband were like."

"Who's Katherine?" asked Tiffany.

"Grandma Katherine. She was very young in nineteen fifty-five, and she was about to give birth to Annie, Kate's mother."

"Oh, okay."

"Anyway, if Auntie Sarah had been keeping journals for a long time, why would she bother to write about that stuff? She wouldn't really need to."

"That's true."

"So what I think is that Auntie Sarah had been looking through the books on the shelves, just as I had, and she found this blank book and decided to keep a journal. Since it was new to her, she wrote about general things at first. But after a while she began to write about other things."

"Like blending?" suggested Tiffany.

"Yes. And about things that interested her."

"What kinds of things?"

"Well, spiders, for one."

"Really? Spiders?"

Annabelle nodded. "Nature in general, I guess. But how much nature could she find indoors? There wasn't even a cat in the house then. So Auntie Sarah mostly saw spiders and insects. And she seemed to like spiders quite a bit. She studied them and drew them."

"How did she study them?" asked Tiffany.

"She just . . . observed them. She drew pictures of them, and wrote all sorts of things about them. Like what kinds of webs they spun and how big they were and what they ate. You know what I learned? That different spiders spin different kinds of webs. And Auntie Sarah wrote that not all spiders spin webs. Some catch their prey in other ways. I don't know whether Auntie Sarah ever saw any of those spiders, though."

"How would she know about them then?"

"That's what I was wondering. I think maybe she found a magazine article or a book about spiders. Or maybe she heard a radio program about them. There's a lot of other spider information in her journal—things Auntie Sarah wouldn't have been able to learn just by observing spiders."

"Like what?"

"Like there are around one hundred and

fifty *thousand* species of spiders." Tiffany raised her eyebrows. "And all spiders are carnivores," Annabelle continued.

"Ew," said Tiffany.

"Spiders are not insects. They are arachnids. Insects have antennae and six legs, and spiders have no antennae and eight legs. Also, most spiders have eight eyes."

Tiffany had edged closer to Annabelle. "Show me some of the parts about spiders," she said.

Annabelle flipped back through the journal. "Here," she said. "She's writing about spiders that spin orb webs and spiders that spin tangled webs and spiders that make funnel webs. She even tried to draw pictures of the webs. She took the journal with her sometimes when she went exploring. Look, here's one of her drawings. See? She labeled some of the parts of the spider."

The caption under Auntie Sarah's drawing read COMMON GARDEN SPIDER.

"Garden spider? How would she know about garden spiders?" asked Tiffany.

"I don't know. Like I said, maybe she found a magazine or something."

There are one hundred and fifty
thousand species of spiders

very
common

here are the
some of the
parts of the
spider

carapace

abdomen

notice the way
the eyes are
arranged ...
interesting!

Tegenaria
Duellica
cobweb spider

harmless

descending from the

beautiful.

"Do you remember your aunt talking
about spiders?"

Annabelle shook her head. "Well, maybe
a few times. What I mostly remember is that
she would tell me about explorers and scien-
tists and pioneers and politicians. Mostly
women. Women who made a difference."

"I bet you remember those things
because they interested you more than spiders
do."

"Spiders scare me a little," admitted
Annabelle.

"Maybe that's why your aunt didn't talk to
you about the spiders. She didn't want to scare
you."

"Maybe," said Annabelle. "But I think
she just didn't want me to know about her
explorations."

Annabelle and Tiffany studied the picture of the common garden spider. Then
Annabelle turned the page.

"Here's another drawing," she said. "It's
of a . . ." Annabelle paused. "Look at those
long words. It's a *Tegenaria duellica*, the cobweb
spider. Oh, it's so huge and hairy."

"But harmless," added Tiffany, peering

this one
surprised me near the sink

at the journal. She turned a page. "Here's a
. . . a . . . an a-ran-e-o-morph." Tiffany
sounded out the word. Then she peered down
at the faded writing on the page. "It's a more
advanced spider," she read.

"Look at all the parts," said Annabelle.
"Patella, trochanter, chelicera. I've seen lots
of spiders, but I don't think they looked like
this."

Annabelle read from the page opposite
the drawing. *"Arachnids have sense organs
that—"*

"Do we really have to read all this?" asked
Tiffany. "This stuff is boring. And it isn't
going to help us find your aunt."

Annabelle frowned. "You never know
what might be a clue," she said.

"But let's just skip to the end of the journal. Let's see what's on the last page."

Annabelle hesitated. "All right," she said
at last.

Tiffany took the book from Annabelle
and opened to the last page. "Hey, it's empty.
Nothing is written on it."

"Probably because she disappeared. She
didn't get to finish the journal. Here. Look."

Annabelle turned the pages backward until she came to one that was half filled. "This is the end," she said.

"Is she still writing about spiders?"

"It says, '. . . *find a way into the attic.*' It starts in the middle of a sentence," Annabelle pointed out. She continued reading. *"Needed time when humans would be away for a while. Over weekend when they were gone for three days made two trips to attic. Timed them. Think I can get to attic, explore, and be back in just under three hours. Doesn't allow for much exploration, but it's something. Could even go to attic on a weekday morning if everyone is out and if attic door is open. If so, could go to attic several times a week."* Annabelle stopped reading. "Several times a week!" she exclaimed. "Heavens." She turned back to the diary. *"Could go for longer periods of time at night. Will attempt next trip tomorrow morning if possible. Good night, dear diary."*

"That's the end of the journal?" said Tiffany.

"That's the end."

"Well, she must be in the attic, then. It's simple."

Suddenly Annabelle felt uncomfortable.

"It seems a little too simple," she said, frowning.

"What do you mean?"

"Well . . . Auntie Sarah has been missing for decades. And all we had to do was find this journal and read the last page, and . . . ?"

"What? What?" asked Tiffany.

Annabelle frowned harder than ever. "I'm not sure." She turned back several pages of the journal. Then she flipped to the last page again. She squinted at the writing. "Tiffany, does this look like exactly the same writing to you?"

"Exactly the same as what?"

"As the writing at the beginning of the journal."

Tiffany took the book from Annabelle. She opened it to the first page and studied the writing. Then she turned to the middle and studied the writing there. Then she turned to the last page. "Annabelle! It doesn't look the same!"

"But . . . but . . . how . . ."

Annabelle and Tiffany stared at each other.

"What would that mean?" Tiffany finally asked. "That it isn't Auntie Sarah's writing?"

"And if it isn't, whose is it?"

"Oh, it must be your aunt's writing," said Tiffany after a moment. "Her hand was probably getting tired. Or something."

"Or maybe it *is* someone else's writing."

"Annabelle, are you playing a trick on me?" Tiffany pulled away from Annabelle, looking cross. "That isn't very nice. I don't like having tricks played on me."

"No, no! Honest! It isn't me."

"Then who could it be?"

A shiver ran down Annabelle's spine. "I have no idea. Nobody even knows I found the journal. At least I don't think anyone does."

"Have you kept it hidden?"

"Yes! Very well hidden."

"The whole time?"

"The whole time."

"I bet Bobby found it."

"Maybe. But he couldn't have written in it."

"Why not?"

"Have you ever seen Bobby's writing? He only writes with pencil, he presses really hard, and he makes huge letters."

Tiffany looked at the writing on the last page of the journal. It was dainty and thin and written in blue ink. "I guess it's not Bobby's," she said. "Let's see where the new writing begins."

Annabelle and Tiffany turned to the second to the last page of the journal.

"It begins here," said Annabelle, pointing to the bottom of the page. "The last sentences in Auntie Sarah's handwriting say *The humans will be waking soon. Time to get ready for another day. Good night, dear diary.'* And then all that stuff about going to the attic was added."

"This is so weird," said Tiffany.

"Spooky," said Annabelle.

"Well, I don't know whose writing that is," said Tiffany, "but I know something else."

"What?" cried Annabelle.

"Your aunt must be in the attic. And someone wants us to look for her there."

Once again Annabelle shivered. Even so, she looked squarely at Tiffany and said, "All right."

CHAPTER TWELVE

The Dolls Go Visiting

*A*NNABELLE and Tiffany were not able to go to the attic right away, of course. They knew they would have to plan such a trip carefully.

"I don't even know where the attic is," said Annabelle.

"You don't?" said Tiffany.

Annabelle shook her head. "I've barely left my house, you know."

"Well, an attic is always upstairs somewhere," said Tiffany wisely.

"Somewhere above this floor?"

"Probably. Or it could be at the back

of this floor. But it wouldn't be down-stairs."

"How are we ever going to convince our parents to let us go to the attic?" asked Annabelle.

"We could just say we're going on an-other exploration. We don't have to say exactly where we're going."

"Oh, that doesn't seem quite right. Besides, we're still in trouble for coming home late the last time."

Tiffany scrunched up her face. She gazed across the room at the Barbie camper. She could just see Uncle Doll sitting in it, staring at the ceiling. Barbie sat nearby, staring at nothing.

"Well, I'll think of something," said Tiffany. "Anyway, I guess I better go home now. I'll see you tomorrow night, Annabelle."

"Maybe my family can come over to your house tomorrow night," said Annabelle brightly. "Since we missed our visit with you."

The next morning, the moment Papa announced that the coast was clear, two things happened at once. Uncle Doll scrambled down the step stool and headed for the Barbie camper, and Annabelle said, "Mama, could we visit the Funcrafts tonight? We didn't get to go before—"

"Because you were in Doll State!" said Bobby gleefully.

"—and we don't want to be rude. Last night Tiffany asked me again when we're going to come over." (Annabelle didn't mind bending the truth a bit.)

Mama hesitated and hemmed and hawed and cleared her throat a couple of times, but finally Annabelle convinced her and Papa to go to the Funcrafts'. Nanny decided to stay behind with Baby Betsy, which Annabelle thought was all right, but

she was determined that Uncle Doll not miss out on the fun, so she paid him a visit at the camper.

"Please, please, please? You have to come with us tonight. *Please?*" she said to Uncle Doll, who was lying on a lounge chair outside the camper. "I really want you to come. It will be fun. You like Tiffany. I know you do. And you won't have to talk to Mama and Papa very much. Okay?"

In the end, Uncle Doll agreed.

Very crossly.

Annabelle was thrilled. She couldn't wait to see the Funcrafts' house, and she had an idea about the attic that she wanted to discuss with Tiffany.

That night, the Dolls waited until Kate and the Palmers were asleep. To Annabelle's relief, The Captain was not in Kate's room. And so, the moment Papa announced that the coast was clear, Annabelle scrambled for the stool. She and Bobby and Uncle Doll started down.

"Travel safely!" called Nanny, who stood at the edge of the parlor propping up Baby Betsy.

"Righto!" replied Papa as he and Mama made their way down the top step.

Annabelle landed on the floor first and helped Bobby and Uncle Doll down. She put her finger to her lips, and Bobby nodded. He knew they must be absolutely silent. Then Bobby reached up and took the flowers Mama was carrying. When everyone was safely on the floor, Annabelle and Uncle Doll led the way across Kate's bedroom. The Dolls ran to the nearest wall and slid along it, facing into the room, until they reached the door. Then Annabelle turned and peered into the hallway. She saw no shining eyes. She heard no rumbling purr. Nothing but darkness and quiet. Holding Uncle Doll's hand, she ran to Nora's room as fast she could, her family close behind.

At Nora's doorway, Annabelle stopped short, her heart pounding. She had a horrible feeling that when she peeked around the corner she would find herself staring directly into The Captain's face. But she knew that was silly. She had found that the things she actually worried about rarely happened. When bad things did happen, they took her by surprise.

Annabelle marched boldly into Nora's room—and gasped. There in the glow of Nora's night-light was The Captain. And there were Dad Funcraft and Tiffany dancing from side to side in front of him. The Dolls stiffened. They watched as The Captain shot out a paw to try to catch Dad, and he dodged it. Annabelle let out a tiny screech. Tiffany looked up when she heard this, and The Captain's paw nearly came down on her head. But she leaped out of The Captain's reach, giggling. "Silly cat!" she cried. Then, "Hey, everybody! The Dolls are here!"

Cringing, Annabelle glanced at Nora and saw that she was sleeping soundly. Then she looked around the room for the Funcrafts' house. There it was, on the floor next to Nora's bed, pink and white like an enormous plastic birthday cake. Annabelle realized she was looking at it from the side. The back was open and furniture lay strewn about amidst odd pieces of Nora's clothing, several farm animals, and a scattering of Legos. Extending from the back of the house

was a pink-stoned terrace with a shallow pool of dark liquid in the center. Nora's handiwork, Annabelle guessed. Grape soda, maybe. She peered around to the front. Four windows, one upstairs and one downstairs on each side of the house, framed two tall white columns between which was the front door, and above it, a balcony.

Annabelle was fascinated by the house, but The Captain demanded her immediate attention. He was crouched between Annabelle and the house. In fact, he was between Annabelle and the rest of the room.

"Maybe we should leave," Annabelle whispered to Bobby.

But Tiffany turned then and called, "Come on in! Don't worry about The Captain. He won't bother you. He just likes to play. He never catches us."

"Well—" began Annabelle.

"Hello! Welcome!" said Mom Funcraft, waving as she sloshed across the patio. "Let me get him out of your way." She turned and dashed into Nora's closet. The Captain tore after her, but he didn't fit through the mostly closed door. So he stuck his paw through the crack and batted at Mom. He couldn't reach her, though, and Annabelle could hear her laughing.

"Isn't she something?" said Dad, beaming at his wife. Then, "Come in, come in," he said to the Dolls.

Annabelle didn't know what to say. She and her family huddled in the doorway.

Tiffany approached them. "Really. Don't be afraid of The Captain. I promise he's just playing."

From the closet came the sound of a scuffle and more laughter. Tiffany ignored it. "Why don't you go play with Bailey?" she said to Bobby.

Bobby looked toward the closet. "I don't know. . . ."

At that moment, Uncle Doll stepped hesitatingly into Nora's room. He looked from The Captain to the Funcrafts' dream house and back to The Captain. Then he turned and looked behind him into the dark hallway. Annabelle could see how nervous he was.

"Uncle Doll—" she started to say.

But Uncle Doll had begun to run. Not

into the dark hallway, where he would have had to make the long trip back to Kate's room by himself. Instead, he was dashing across Nora's floor, heading for the safety of the dream house.

The Captain turned and saw him. The next thing Annabelle knew, her uncle was clamped between The Captain's teeth. "Uncle Doll!" she shrieked.

The Captain leaped onto Nora's bed.

The Dolls and the Funcrafts stared. For several long, horrible seconds they watched as The Captain shook his prize. Then Papa Doll tore into Nora's room and began jumping up and down. He waved his arms in the air. "Captain! Oh, Captain!" he shouted, and not one single doll told him to keep his voice down. "Captain!" Papa called again.

The Captain stopped shaking Uncle Doll. He looked at Papa, then jumped to the floor, where Uncle Doll tumbled from his mouth. Instantly, The Captain snatched up Papa and ran under Nora's bed.

Mama fainted.

In the confusion, Dad Funcraft slid Mama Doll out of the doorway, and the Dolls and the Funcrafts gathered around her. But Annabelle kept her eye on The Captain.

And she was the only one who saw him streak through the doorway, Papa dangling from his mouth, and disappear down the hall.

"Uh-oh," said Annabelle, and everyone turned to look at her.

CHAPTER THIRTEEN

Where's Papa?

*N*ORA'S ROOM was a wreck, and Annabelle was positive the Doll Code of Honor had been broken. Things had been moved. Mom Funcraft had tracked grape soda across the rug. The paper flowers had been trampled. Dolls that didn't belong in the room were there. Worst of all, one doll was missing.

Annabelle surveyed the room while the grown-ups

revived Mama Doll. She found that she was shaking, but not, she realized, with fear. Annabelle was furious. She couldn't remember the last time she had been quite so angry. Maybe she had never been this angry before.

Papa had been carried off by The Captain, and it was Tiffany's fault. Tiffany with her "Don't worry about The Captain," and her "He never catches us," and her "I promise he's just playing."

Annabelle glared at Tiffany. Tiffany was talking quietly to Bobby and Bailey. When she glanced up and saw Annabelle looking at her, she joined her in the doorway. "I—I'm sorry, Annabelle," she said. "I really didn't think . . . I mean, The Captain has never . . . We've been playing with him almost every night since we got here."

Annabelle continued to glare at Tiffany.

"I—I know you're mad—" Tiffany began to say.

Annabelle nodded.

"Well . . . I said I was sorry."

"I know." Annabelle looked

down at her feet. She looked across the room at the grown-ups. Then she let out a big sigh.

"Look, if you're just going to be mad—"

"Tiffany, let's not fight," Annabelle interrupted her. "Anyway, this is partly our fault. I mean, my family and I decided to come over here. You didn't force us to do that."

"No."

"So let's just do what we have to do. Together. And the first thing we have to do is put Nora's room back in order. Quickly," she added, looking at the clock on the wall. "And the rest of my family has to go home. Then you and I will start looking for Papa."

"SELMP," said Tiffany.

"Exactly," said Annabelle. "It's a good thing we're prepared for something like this."

By now Uncle Doll had helped Mama rise shakily to her feet. "Papa saved me," he said breathlessly. "He saved my life."

"He loves you," said Mama. "You're family."

"But I blamed you for . . . And then I lost my temper, and I moved out."

"Everyone quarrels," said Mama.

Annabelle wanted to say, "*We* never used

to." But there wasn't time for a discussion. "Come on, everybody," she said, shooing her family toward the door. "We have a lot to do. And look at the time. Uncle Doll, Bobby—you take Mama home."

"And Mom and Dad," said Tiffany, "you and Bailey clean up Nora's room."

"What are you going to do?" Mama Doll asked Annabelle.

"Tiffany and I are going to look for Papa."

"Oh, but you can't," said Mama in a small voice.

"Yes, we can. And we are going to."

"Can we come?" asked Bobby and Bailey.

"Nope. This is for girls only," said Tiffany.

"Besides, if too many people go looking, it will get confusing," said Annabelle. "We're just going to search quickly, and come back before the Palmers wake up."

Bailey and Bobby started to protest, but Annabelle said sternly, "And we mean it!" which she had heard Papa say any number of times.

So the Dolls hurried down the hallway,

and the Funcrafts began to clean up, and Annabelle and Tiffany huddled briefly by the corner of Nora's bureau.

"Where shall we look first?" asked Tiffany.

"Well, The Captain might be nearby, maybe in Kate's parents' room. But I don't think we should search there. At least not right now. That would be too risky."

"He could just as easily have run downstairs," said Tiffany. "Maybe we should start there."

"Okay," agreed Annabelle.

Annabelle and Tiffany searched the Palmers' dining room and kitchen before they got nervous about the time and returned to their homes.

On her way across Kate's room Annabelle did a quick check under all the furniture to see whether The Captain was hiding nearby with Papa, but he isn't in sight.

"Any luck?" called Mama as soon as she saw Annabelle.

"No."

The next day was

Saturday and at least one of the Palmers was home all day long. Annabelle, stuck in the dollhouse, worried that Kate would peek inside and wonder why Papa was no longer seated at the table where she had left him the night before. Then she worried that Papa had been injured. Had one of his arms or legs been smashed? Had his *head* been smashed? Annabelle could do nothing but wait until bedtime, when she and Tiffany could continue their search.

That night, the first night without Papa, it was Uncle Doll who called, "The coast is clear!" when he had decided the Palmers' house was dark and silent enough to mean that all the humans were fast asleep. Annabelle looked at him sitting in the parlor with Mama and Nanny and Bobby and Baby Betsy. She took a picture of them with her mind. Then she made a dash for the stool and was waiting in the hall when Tiffany appeared.

The girls made their way downstairs and searched the TV room, the front hallway, and Grandma Katherine's bathroom. They wanted to search Grandma Katherine's bedroom, but were afraid.

"We'll save the worst rooms for last," said Tiffany. "Tomorrow we'll search the living room."

The girls had avoided the living room because The Captain's bed was there, but now Annabelle had an idea. "Tiffany!" she exclaimed. "I know I said I didn't want to go near The Captain's bed, but I just thought of something. Remember when Nora threw me downstairs and I landed on his bed?"

"Yes."

"Well, I found a lot of stuff in the bed."

"Like what?"

"A couple of Nora's plastic animals, and a toy mouse, and a doll Kate made for Nora."

"So?" said Tiffany.

"Well, don't you see?" Annabelle felt impatient. "The Captain hides little things in his bed. Maybe that's where he took Papa."

Tiffany gasped and put her hand to her mouth. "Oh, Annabelle. I bet you're right. First thing tomorrow night we'll search his bed."

"If he's not in it," said Annabelle.

When Annabelle and Tiffany met in the hallway the next night, Annabelle was cross. "The

Captain isn't on the end of Kate's bed," she told Tiffany.

"I thought you didn't *like* him to be there."

"I don't. But if he isn't there, then he might be sleeping on his bed. And if he's on his bed, then we can't search it tonight."

"That's true, but he could also be somewhere else in the house," Tiffany pointed out reasonably. "So let's go downstairs and look."

Annabelle and Tiffany made the long trip down the living room stairs. When they reached the bottom, Annabelle took Tiffany's hand and said, "Shh," as softly as she was able.

Tiffany nodded. Then the girls began to tiptoe to the bed. In case The Captain might be nearby, they took a long route around the room, walking along the little path between the wall and the edge of the rug. When they drew near to the old sweater, Annabelle stood still and peered at it.

"Can you see anything?" whispered Tiffany.

"Not much."

The girls stepped a bit closer.

"How about now?" asked Tiffany.

"Nope. Not yet."

They tiptoed closer.

Suddenly Annabelle grabbed Tiffany's arm. "He's there! The Captain is right there!" It was all Annabelle could do not to shriek.

Tiffany leaned forward. Then she did something that astounded Annabelle. She ran to the edge of the sweater and kicked at it. Nothing happened. She kicked again. Nothing.

"He couldn't be there," Tiffany announced. "He would have felt that for sure. I think you just saw a shadow, Annabelle. Come on. Let's explore the sweater."

Cautiously, the girls crawled onto the sweater. Tiffany had been right. The Captain wasn't there. For five long minutes the girls felt around in the dark. Annabelle found the cow and the chicken again, but not the little doll. Tiffany found the mouse and wanted to take it back to the dream house with her, but Annabelle told her not to. Then Tiffany found a tiny plastic house that Annabelle thought had come from Kate's Monopoly game. But after several more minutes, they still had not found Papa Doll.

"Are we *sure* he isn't here?" said Annabelle, poking at the sweater with her foot.

"Pretty sure," replied Tiffany. "I'm sorry, Annabelle."

Annabelle looked at her feet. She didn't say anything.

"Well, we haven't searched everywhere," said Tiffany. "We can't give up yet. He could even be in the attic with Auntie Sarah."

"I guess."

"If we go to the attic, we might find both of them at once."

After a long pause, Annabelle said, "I don't know . . ." She paused again.

"What? What are you thinking?" asked Tiffany.

"I just have a feeling Papa isn't in the attic. Wherever the attic is, I don't think the Palmers go to it very often. And I'm pretty sure The Captain can't get into it by himself, so I don't think he took Papa there in the middle of the night when the Palmers were asleep. I guess he could have taken him later, but probably not."

"So you think your father is somewhere else in the house."

"Yes. Somewhere we haven't searched yet. Or somewhere that we can't get to."

"Then we just have to keep searching."

"I know. I guess I was hoping it would be

easier than this. I wanted SELMP to do a really great job. I wanted us to find Papa— *snap*—like that! And then go to the attic and find Auntie Sarah—*snap*—like that! And we would be heroes."

Tiffany smiled. "We're going to be heroes," she said. "Don't get discouraged, Annabelle. I don't think your aunt would have. She would have thought up a plan—"

"*We* thought up a plan," Annabelle pointed out. "We thought of searching The Captain's bed. But it didn't work."

"So we need another plan."

Annabelle and Tiffany slid off of The Captain's bed and sat down under a small chest of drawers. They thought and thought. Annabelle thought until she got a little headache. At last she said, "The only thing I can think of—and maybe this is really dumb, because we'll have to hang around The Captain—but the only thing I can think of is to follow The Captain. If he's hidden Papa somewhere, or dropped him somewhere, maybe he'll go back for him."

"Well," said Tiffany, "I don't exactly want to go following The Captain around, but you know, Annabelle, I think you have a very good idea. I think that's exactly what we should do."

"When?" asked Annabelle.

"Tomorrow night. Try to keep track of The Captain during the day tomorrow if you see him, okay?"

Annabelle nodded. Then she put her hands on Tiffany's shoulders and said solemnly, "United for SELMP."

And Tiffany put her hands on Annabelle's shoulders and said solemnly, "United for SELMP."

If Annabelle had known that she and Tiffany would follow The Captain for four nights, she might not have mentioned her plan at all. After the third night she said, "Tiffany, I don't think this is working. All The Captain does is walk from one bed to another and sleep for a while—his sweater bed, the end of Kate's bed, under Grandma Katherine's bed. This is silly. I think we're wasting time. Besides, our luck won't last forever. I can't believe Kate hasn't looked in the dollhouse yet."

"Let's just try it one more night," said
Tiffany. "If we don't find anything interesting, we'll think of something else. Okay?"

"Okay," agreed Annabelle.

On the fourth night, which was the sixth
night after The Captain had taken Papa, the
girls met in the hallway outside Kate's room as
soon as they felt it was safe.

"Have you seen The Captain?" asked
Tiffany.

"Not in a while. But I think he's downstairs."

Annabelle and Tiffany made their way to
the living room.

"There he is. He's on his bed,"
Annabelle whispered a moment later. "I can
see him. I'm sure of it."

"I see him, too," Tiffany whispered back.

The girls tiptoed around the room until
they reached the couch that was across
from the sweater bed. When they slid under
one end of the couch and lifted the skirt that
ran around the bottom, they could just see
The Captain.

"He's sound asleep," Annabelle observed.

Half an hour later, he was still asleep.

But fifteen minutes after that, he stirred. Tiffany grabbed Annabelle's wrist. The girls inched forward ever so slightly. The Captain sat up. He stretched. He stretched again. Then he eased himself off of the sweater and ambled across the living room. He batted at a little ball as he went by it, and sent it flying. At the edge of the living room he paused. He sat down. He looked to the left. He looked to the right. Then he stood up, turned around, and walked back into the living room. Tiffany nudged Annabelle with her elbow. Annabelle nudged her back. The Captain was acting unusual, and this was interesting.

Annabelle, who by now was crouched under one of the armchairs peeking around the edge of the skirt, peered through the darkness. Not far away stood a tall cupboard with drawers, a heavy old piece of furniture that Annabelle had heard Grandma Katherine call an armoire. The Captain was walking around it. When he reached the back he sat down and began scratching at a corner of it, his tail swishing back and forth across the floor.

Annabelle leaned forward, listening

hard. Tiffany listened, too. Then the girls stared at each other, wide-eyed.

Faintly, very faintly, they could hear a voice from behind the armoire calling, "Shoo, cat. Shoo! Go away, Captain!"

The Captain rose onto his hind legs and reached as far up the armoire as he could. Then he stretched his front paws into the small space between the wall and the back of the armoire. He jumped and batted at something, jumped again. Whatever he wanted he couldn't reach. He slid down until once more he was sitting on the floor. Then he let out a frustrated meow before giving up and leaving the living room altogether.

The moment he was gone Annabelle and Tiffany ran behind the armoire. "Papa?" called Annabelle. "Papa, is that you?"

"Annabelle?" said Papa's voice in surprise.

"Oh, it *is* you! . . . Where are you?"

"I'm up here," said Papa.

Annabelle and Tiffany looked up. There was Papa, wedged into the space behind the armoire, about three feet above their heads.

"Papa! I can't believe we found you. I'm here with Tiffany. We've been looking and looking for you! We've been looking for days."

"How did you get way up there?" asked Tiffany.

"The Captain dropped me down from the top. But there isn't much space back here and I got stuck partway down. I'm glad I didn't land on the floor, but I don't know how to free myself."

"Okay," said Tiffany. "Don't worry. We'll help you. I'll think of something. Annabelle, you stay here with your father. I'll be back as soon as I can." Tiffany ran for the stairs.

Annabelle gazed up at Papa. He looked down at her. "What do you suppose Tiffany is going to do?" he asked.

"I haven't the faintest idea," replied Annabelle.

CHAPTER FOURTEEN

The Funcrafts to the Rescue

OR WHAT seemed like hours, but was probably no more than three quarters of an hour, Annabelle sat below Papa Doll. She talked to him, told him about the events of the past few days (although she didn't mention SELMP—that was private, just between her and Tiffany), and listened to his story of being carried off by The Captain and dropped behind the armoire.

"It was terrifying," said Papa. And Annabelle felt horrible. Papa spent his life avoiding excitement, wanting only to reside quietly in the dollhouse. Then Annabelle had decided to change things, had made him venture out of the safety of his house, and look what had happened.

By the time she heard Tiffany on the stairs, Annabelle had apologized six times to Papa.

When Tiffany appeared in the living room, she was not alone. Mom, Dad, and Bailey Funcraft were following her, carrying a rope. Tiffany held one end of it, Mom held the other, and Dad and Bailey propped up the middle so that the rope never touched the floor and didn't make a sound.

"What's that for?" asked Annabelle, straining to see in the dark. "And where's Baby Britney?"

"She's over at your house," replied Tiffany. "Nanny is watching her. And this rope, which is Kate's jump rope, by the way, is for . . . well, you'll see."

"What? What?" said Annabelle.

"Just watch. I have a great idea."

Annabelle stood back and watched.

The Funcrafts must have discussed their rescue operation on the way down the stairs, because now they set to work without saying a word. First Mom and Bailey tied one end of the rope, which was old and had lost its handles, around Tiffany's middle. This was difficult since the rope was very thick, but at last they fashioned a tight, if clumsy, knot. Then, with the rope securely around her waist, Tiffany approached the armoire. She reached for the brass pull on the lowest drawer and hoisted herself up. She looked behind her at her family and gave them the thumbs-up sign.

"What's going on down there?" Papa called to Annabelle.

"I'm not sure," she replied. "Tiffany's climbing up the front of the armoire with a rope. I guess we'll find out the rest in a minute."

Tiffany reached for the pull on the second drawer and once again hoisted herself up. Higher and higher she climbed, the rope trailing behind her. At last she scrambled onto the top of the armoire. She scurried to the back and peered over the edge. "Mr. Doll! Helloooo!" she called.

Annabelle saw her father look up in surprise. "Tiffany," he exclaimed. "That was so fast."

"Well, I don't have to worry about breaking," she replied.

And Annabelle felt envious, thinking of how careful she had to be with her china body.

From the other side of the armoire Dad Funcraft called, "Okay, Tiffany. We'll hold on to this end of the rope and you drop over the edge to Mr. Doll."

There was a moment of silence. Then Tiffany said, "You know what? That isn't going to work after all. The rope isn't long enough. It just reached up here. I think I'll have to pull it up, and tie the other end to the top drawer pull."

Tiffany did so, with amazing speed. Then she stood at the back of the armoire and once again looked down at Papa. "Okay, Mr. Doll, here I come!" she called. And she leaped over the edge.

Annabelle had barely had time to pray that the knot would hold, when she heard Papa say

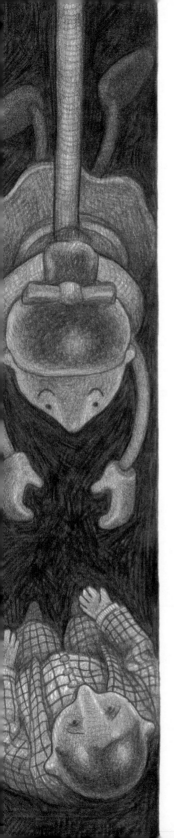

"Oof," as Tiffany landed on him.

"Is everything all right?" Annabelle called. She felt something touch her elbow and realized that Mom, Dad, and Bailey had joined her.

"Yes. Fine," said Papa.

"It's a tight fit," added Tiffany, who had braced herself between the wall and the armoire.

For the next few minutes all Annabelle could hear were grunts and bumps and little scraping sounds. Then she heard Papa say, "That did it! I'm free."

"Hold on tight, then," said Tiffany. "I'm going to let go now. We should drop right to the floor."

But they didn't. The rope, stretching across the top of the armoire before trailing down the back, was not long enough to reach the floor. Tiffany and Papa dropped another foot and hung there.

"Now what?" asked Papa nervously.

"We'll have to jump," said Tiffany, starting to untie the rope.

"And I'll have to climb the drawer pulls, untie the other end of the rope, and throw it down," said Mom Funcraft cheerfully. "We can't leave a thing like that hanging around."

"I'm afraid to jump," said Papa, as Tiffany removed the rope and they braced themselves against the wall.

Mom reached the top of the armoire, untied the rope, tossed it to the floor, and climbed down again, and still Papa hadn't moved.

"Papa, you *have* to jump," Annabelle cried. "It's getting late. We have to go home now. All of us."

"I'll jump first," said Tiffany. She dropped to the floor with a small clatter.

"Well, then, here I come," said Papa shakily.

Annabelle heard the crack when he landed.

"I've broken my leg!" said Papa.

Annabelle and the Funcrafts didn't waste another second. They ran to Papa and dragged him to the front of the armoire. Annabelle was just thinking that they were being awfully noisy when she heard the *pad, pad, pad* of The Captain.

"Danger! Danger!" cried Annabelle.

The dolls scattered, except for Papa, who couldn't stand up.

In an instant he was clamped between The Captain's jaws once again, and The Captain trotted off, looking smug.

"Help!" cried Papa.

"Follow them!" cried Dad.

Annabelle and the Funcrafts ran after The Captain, but skidded to a halt when they saw a pair of feet in fuzzy slippers approach.

"Hide!" hissed Annabelle. She and the Funcrafts dove behind a chair. Annabelle peered out.

"Captain!" exclaimed a startled voice. The feet belonged to Grandma Katherine, who turned on a light. "What have

you got in your mouth? . . . . Why, it's Papa Doll. Naughty kitty!"

"Mother? Is everything all right?" Now Mrs. Palmer appeared, walking sleepily down the stairs. "What's going on?"

"Oh, I couldn't sleep and I was going to the kitchen for some tea," began Grandma Katherine, "when I nearly bumped into The Captain, who was running around with *this* in his mouth." She held up Papa.

Mrs. Palmer scowled. "All right. I believe The Captain will have to stay downstairs at night. No more sleeping in Kate's room. At least for a while."

Yes! exclaimed Annabelle silently.

Mrs. Palmer and Grandma Katherine examined Papa under a lamp. "Oh, look. His leg is cracked," said Mrs. Palmer.

"I can fix it, though," said Grandma Katherine. "All it needs is a little glue. I'll do it tomorrow and put Papa back in the dollhouse while Kate is at school. She won't even know what happened."

* * *

Annabelle and the Funcrafts remained motionless behind the chair until the Palmers' house was quiet again. Annabelle was jubilant. The Captain had been shut in the kitchen. And he wouldn't roam the second floor at night. At least not for a long time, she suspected. Better yet, Papa would be returned to the dollhouse the very next day.

The dolls began the climb up the stairs. Annabelle and Tiffany hung back. They pulled each other up the steps while Mom, Dad, and Bailey scurried ahead of them.

"What made you think of the rope?" Annabelle asked, impressed.

"It just came to me," Tiffany replied.

"Well, it was a great idea." Annabelle paused. "I don't know how Papa would have gotten down without you."

"You were the one who figured out how to look for him," Tiffany pointed out. "That was brilliant."

Annabelle grinned. But then she added, "It almost didn't work."

"But in the end it did. That's what counts."

When they reached the top of the stairs, Annabelle and the Funcrafts ran to Kate's room, climbed the stool, and told the Dolls the wonderful news. Bobby asked a dozen questions. Nanny put her hand over her heart, and Mama nearly fainted again.

"He'll be home tomorrow?" Mama kept saying.

"That's what Grandma Katherine said," Annabelle reported.

Dad Funcraft looked across Kate's room at her clock. "We better leave," he said. "The Palmers will be getting up soon."

"Well, we'll come visit you," Mama promised, "now that we won't have to worry about The Captain. We'll come as soon as Papa is back and his leg has dried. We can have a celebration."

"Mama? Can I walk Tiffany home?" asked Annabelle.

"Just as far as Kate's door," Mama replied.

Annabelle put her hand in Tiffany's. "Let's go," she said.

At the doorway, Tiffany told her family to go home ahead of her. "I'll be right there. I promise. I just want to talk to Annabelle for a second."

When Annabelle and Tiffany were standing in the shadows by Kate's door, Tiffany said, "SELMP did a pretty good job."

"This assignment was a success," Annabelle agreed proudly.

"Now it's time to go back to our first assignment."

"Auntie Sarah?" said Annabelle.

"Auntie Sarah."

Annabelle nodded solemnly. She and Tiffany put their hands on each other's shoulders. "United for SELMP," they said.

Tiffany turned to leave then but Annabelle caught her hand. "There's one other thing," she whispered. "We have to find out who has been writing in Auntie Sarah's journal."

Annabelle didn't have a chance to look at the journal until the next night. After she left Tiffany, she had just barely returned to the dollhouse before Kate's alarm clock went off. In a flash, the Doll family resumed the positions in which Kate had left them nearly a week earlier, the last time she had played in the dollhouse. They were still in them when, not long after Kate had left for school, Annabelle heard footsteps on the stairs. Moments later, Grandma Katherine entered Kate's room with Papa Doll cradled gently in her hands.

Annabelle didn't move, but she lowered her eyes ever so slightly for a better view.

"Well, now," Grandma Katherine said as she stood before the dollhouse. "What an adventure you had, Papa. Your leg should be as good as new very quickly, though."

Grandma Katherine placed Papa on the couch in the parlor. Then she left Kate's room.

Annabelle listened to her footsteps. She heard them pad down the hallway, then creak down the stairs. When she was fairly certain that Grandma Katherine had reached the bottom step, she cried softly, "Papa!"

And Mama murmured, "Is your leg *truly* all right?"

Annabelle could not help herself. She leaped up and ran for the stairs, pulling Bobby behind her. "It'll just be for a few minutes," she called over her shoulder before Nanny could protest.

She needn't have bothered. Nanny followed her down the stairs. Uncle Doll hurried out of his room. Everyone (except Baby Betsy, who was asleep) gathered around Papa. He stood up to show the Dolls that his leg was fine. Or nearly. It needed to dry a bit longer.

Mama hugged him.

Nanny kissed his cheek.

Annabelle and Bobby hugged him.

Then Uncle Doll held out his hand and shook Papa Doll's. "I'm sorry," he said. "I apologize."

"I apologize, too. I think we both said some things we didn't mean."

"We had a disagreement," said Uncle Doll.

Papa glanced across the room at the Barbie camper. "Are you—?" he started to say.

"No," Uncle Doll interrupted him. "I moved back home again. I miss my room. And Barbie's furniture isn't terribly comfortable."

Bobby stepped forward and touched the leg of Papa's pants. "Can I see the crack?" he asked.

"Bobby!" exclaimed Nanny.

But Papa lifted the leg of his trousers and pointed out the crack. It was no thicker than a hair. A wave of relief washed over Annabelle.

After a few more hugs, and after Papa had described four times how it felt to be clamped between a cat's jaws, and after he had told the tale of his adventures from his capture to his rescue, Mama said, "Well, I suppose we should return to—"

"Oh, please just tell us about The Captain's teeth once more. Please?" begged Bobby.

"Tonight," Papa promised.

And the Dolls returned to their positions.

CHAPTER FIFTEEN

Into the Attic

*T*HAT NIGHT Papa didn't wait as long as usual before he announced, "The coast is clear!" The moment the words were out of his mouth the Dolls ran to where he lay in the parlor. Annabelle had been about to reach for the journal, but she joined her family instead.

"Now how do you feel?" was the first thing Mama said to Papa.

"Even better," he replied. "I think the glue is dry."

Papa sat up. Uncle Doll sat next to him. He and Papa smiled at each other.

"We're glad to have you back with us," said Papa. "You're part of the family. You belong here."

"Thank you. Yes. I know," said Uncle Doll, looking more pleased than uncomfortable.

"Now the whole family is together," said Annabelle, "except for, well, you know . . ."

"Let's not talk about that tonight," said Bobby, glancing at the adults.

Annabelle knew he didn't want any fighting on Papa's first night at home again. And neither did Annabelle. But she did want to find Auntie Sarah. So a few minutes later she returned to the nursery. She opened Auntie Sarah's journal and flipped to the last page on which there was writing.

She gasped.

A new paragraph had been added. It read, *Made another trip to the attic this morning. Wish humans would leave door to attic stairs open more often. But they usually close it. It's just next to Katherine's bedroom. Perhaps a draught comes in when the door is open.*

Annabelle dropped the journal. She

didn't even finish reading the entry. She now knew two things. One: the way to the attic was up a staircase next to a bedroom, which was probably the room in which Kate's parents now slept. Two: someone knew that Annabelle had found the journal, was writing in it, wanted Annabelle to look for Auntie Sarah in the attic, and was telling her the way to the attic.

Annabelle clattered down the staircase, not even bothering to be quiet. "I have to find Tiffany!" she cried as she skidded into the parlor. "It's an emergency. I'll be back later." And she began scrambling down the stool without waiting for her parents or Nanny or Uncle Doll to answer her. She had flown across Kate's room and was rounding the corner into the hall when she crashed into another moving object.

Oh, no, please don't let me be in Doll State again, thought Annabelle. And then she saw that she had run into Tiffany. The girls straightened up quickly and flattened themselves against the wall.

"You won't guess what I found!" exclaimed Annabelle, gasping a little, just as

Tiffany whispered, "It's time for our next mission."

"What?" they both said.

Then, "You go first," said Tiffany.

"Okay, but not here in the hall." Annabelle pulled Tiffany back into Kate's room and they scurried under her dresser. Then Annabelle told her what she had read in the journal.

"The door next to the Palmers' bedroom?" said Tiffany. "Well, what are we waiting for? Let's go. It's time for our next mission anyway. That's what I was coming to tell you."

"Don't we need supplies or something?" asked Annabelle. "This is our biggest mission yet."

"We'll just explore on this one," replied Tiffany. "If we need supplies we'll come back and get them. First let's see if we can get upstairs."

"Okay." Annabelle led the way along the hall to Kate's parents' room. "Here's their door," she said.

It was partway open. Annabelle peeked inside. The room was dimly lit by moonlight shining through a window. Annabelle could hear the soft sounds of breathing, a clock ticking, blankets rustling.

Tiffany pulled her away—a few steps farther down the hall and they were standing by another door.

"Darn, it's closed," Tiffany whispered loudly.

"I don't think I've ever seen it open," said Annabelle. "Well, not in a long time, anyway. I thought it was a closet door. The Palmers don't like The Captain to go in closets, so they keep the closet doors closed."

"They probably don't want him to go in the attic, either," said Tiffany.

The girls stared at the enormous closed door. Then they looked at each other. And then Annabelle reached out and stuck her hands in the crack under the door. She gripped the door and pulled. And the door swung open a few inches.

"Hey!" cried Tiffany.

"The latch hadn't caught. I just had a feeling . . ." said Annabelle.

"Well, come on!" said Tiffany.

Annabelle and Tiffany slithered behind

the partly open door. The darkness on the other side was much darker than the darkness in the hallway. They could barely see.

"This is scary," Annabelle whispered.

"I know. But there's nothing we can do about it. Maybe there will be moonlight in the attic."

Annabelle let out a small sigh. Then she and Tiffany began feeling their way up the staircase.

"It isn't carpeted," said Annabelle. "This is harder than going up the living room stairs."

"Lots harder," Tiffany agreed as her hands slipped and she toppled back on Annabelle.

But the girls kept going. Annabelle said over and over inside her head, "Here we come, Auntie Sarah. Here we come, Auntie Sarah. We're coming, we're coming, we're coming." She set it to a marching tune, and hummed it to herself as she and Tiffany scaled step after step.

Annabelle felt they had climbed quite a long way when she realized she could see her hands in front of her. "Look, Tiffany," she said. "It's lighter here."

"I think we're almost at the top step."

Sure enough, the girls climbed one more step and Annabelle realized that she could see a bit again—and that ahead of her now stretched a long expanse of rough wooden floor. "Tiffany," she said. "I think we're in the attic."

Tiffany grinned. Then she said, "It's so light in here. It's almost as if it were daytime."

"The light's shining through that window," said Annabelle, pointing.

The girls looked ahead of them at a large window. Moonlight poured in. "It must be a full moon tonight," said Tiffany.

Annabelle turned her attention to the rest of the attic. "It's kind of . . . messy," she said.

"I think attics are supposed to be messy," replied Tiffany.

"But boxes, trunks, junk, stuff . . . How are we going to look for Auntie Sarah?"

"We'll just start," said Tiffany practically. "We don't have much time."

"We'll call as we look," added Annabelle.

Annabelle and Tiffany waded through dust bunnies. They peered around corners of cartons. They crawled under discarded furniture.

"Auntie Sarah!" Annabelle called softly.

"Helloooo! Is anybody up here?" called Tiffany.

They paused frequently to listen, but heard nothing except little twitterings and chirpings and sometimes the wind.

Finally Tiffany said, "Annabelle, I think we better go back. It's getting late."

"No. I don't want to leave. I think she's here. I can *feel* her."

"We'll come back tomorrow night."

Annabelle sighed. "All right."

But at noon the next day, the sun began to fade, and by nightfall rain lashed the windows.

Tiffany showed up just moments after Kate had gone to bed and said sadly, "It will be too dark to search the attic tonight, Annabelle. No moonlight."

"I know. I thought about that all afternoon."

"We'll try tomorrow night if we can."

But the rain stayed. It stayed for days.

"And you know what?" Annabelle said to Tiffany one dark night.

"What?"

"By the time the rain stops, we probably won't have any moonlight to search by. It'll be just a sliver of a moon."

"I wish we had a flashlight," said Tiffany. "I mean a big human flashlight."

"But we—"

"I know, I know. We wouldn't be able to carry it. I was just wishing."

In the end, Annabelle and Tiffany had to wait days and days and days before they could search for Auntie Sarah again. They had to wait until the next night with no clouds and an almost full moon.

"I hope the attic door is still open," said
Annabelle on that night as they hurried down
the hallway. They did not bother to listen for
The Captain, who truly had been banished to
the first floor. The dolls hadn't seen him at
nighttime in weeks.

The door was open. Annabelle and
Tiffany climbed the attic stairs as fast as they
could and stood in the moonlight.

"Let's start at the other end of the room
this time," said Tiffany. So they did.

Once again, they waded through dust
bunnies and peeked around the corners of
cartons. Annabelle even climbed a pile of
musty old clothes, stood atop it, and called,
"Auntie Sarah! Auntie Sarah! It's me,
Annabelle! Where are you?" She listened
intently for an answer, but heard nothing.

Several hours later Annabelle heard a

clock chiming, very faintly, from somewhere downstairs.

"Tiffany!" she exclaimed. "Was that *four* chimes?"

"Yes," replied Tiffany. "Uh-oh."

"We have to leave right now."

The trip down the attic stairs seemed to take forever, since Annabelle and Tiffany had to creep down them very slowly. Without carpeting, their movements made tiny clicks and thumps and clatters. But they managed to return to their homes before the Palmers awoke.

The members of SELMP searched the attic again the next night without any luck. Annabelle began to fear that Auntie Sarah would not be found soon.

"Oh, I just can't bear the thought of waiting for the next full moon," she said to Tiffany.

"Let's try tomorrow night anyway. Maybe there will be enough light to see by."

On the third night of the search, the light had faded, but Annabelle and Tiffany were familiar with the attic, and poked through its hiding places anyway.

"How much time do we have?" Tiffany asked Annabelle after a while.

"I don't know." Annabelle was disentangling her foot from a bit of rag that was caught under the corner of an enormous steamer trunk.

"Look at all the stickers on that trunk," said Tiffany. "Someone sure traveled a lot."

"I bet it was William Seab— Hey!" cried Annabelle. "Hey, *hey,* HEY!" She didn't bother to keep her voice down.

"SHHHH!" said Tiffany.

Annabelle ignored her. "Hey!" she said again.

"What *is* it?"

"This!" exclaimed Annabelle, poking at the rag she had tripped over.

Tiffany bent down to examine it. "Yeah?"

"It's . . ." Annabelle's voice caught. "It's . . . I'm pretty sure it's Auntie Sarah's dress."

Annabelle was standing at a corner of the trunk. With her shoe, she poked at the bit of faded blue fabric. Then she peeked around the corner, and there, between the trunk and the attic wall, the skirt of her dress trapped neatly under the trunk, was Auntie Sarah.

Annabelle gasped. Speechless, she grabbed Tiffany and pulled her to her discovery.

Tiffany stared in horror. "Is *that* your aunt?" she whispered.

"I think so."

The girls stared. Auntie Sarah was covered in dust. Her left hand was chipped. Old cobwebs stretched between the trunk and her dress. Her eyes stared dully ahead.

"Auntie Sarah?" Annabelle said tentatively. She looked into the expressionless eyes. "Auntie Sarah, it's me. It's Annabelle."

Auntie Sarah didn't move.

"Are you sure it's your aunt?" asked Tiffany. "Maybe it's some other doll. I don't think she's alive."

"No. It's Auntie Sarah," replied Annabelle, a sinking feeling in her stomach. "But I think she's in Permanent Doll State."

Tiffany lowered her eyes. "Oh . . . I'm sorry."

Annabelle poked at Auntie Sarah's dress, her chipped hand, the cobwebs. "We might as well leave," she said.

Then she jumped as a loud voice exclaimed, "Are you crazy? After all this time?"

Annabelle stumbled backward against Tiffany.

The doll on the attic floor had spoken.

CHAPTER SIXTEEN

The Dolls Make a Plan

UNTIE SARAH?" Anna-
belle had found herself clutching at Tiffany,
but now she let go and stepped toward the
doll on the floor. "Are you alive? Are you
really alive?"

"I'm coming to," said Auntie Sarah, and
Annabelle remembered a time, years and years
ago, when Grandma Katherine had been playing with her in bed and had forgotten about
her, and Annabelle had slipped down between
the side of the bed and the wall. She had been
wedged there for close to a week, and during
that time had felt groggy and sluggish, like a

frog hibernating at the bottom of a pond. She hadn't been in Doll State, but she had felt as if she had been in another kind of state, one that changed her perception of time, so that when she was finally discovered, she had been surprised to find that six and a half days had passed instead of merely an hour or two.

"Auntie Sarah, we've been looking everywhere for you!"

"We've been searching and searching," added Tiffany. "You don't know me, but I—"

"Is *Amaurobius ferox* nearby?" asked Auntie Sarah sleepily.

"What?" said Annabelle.

"The—the black lace weaver?"

"Um . . ."

"Is that a spider?" asked Tiffany brightly.

"Yes, and I was *so* close to it—"

Annabelle uttered a cry and jumped aside.

"Annabelle, that was forty-five years ago," said Tiffany. "I don't think it's still around."

"Forty-five years ago?" exclaimed Auntie Sarah, sounding both distressed and more awake.

"Yes," said Annabelle.

"But how—"

"Annabelle read your journal," said Tiffany, and Annabelle dug her elbow into Tiffany's side.

"What? Oh, my . . ."

Annabelle knelt beside Auntie Sarah. "Can you sit up?" she asked.

"No. I'm stuck. That's the problem."

"Well, wiggle out of your dress, then," said Tiffany.

"I can't. I've tried and tried, but I'm sewn into it. And part of my sleeve is caught, too. See?"

"Okay. Then we'll pull you out," said Annabelle. "Here, Tiffany. Grab her shoulders."

Annabelle and Tiffany grabbed and pulled. And pulled. And pulled some more. Nothing happened.

"I guess we're not strong enough," said Tiffany at last, eyeing the trunk. "How did you get trapped here anyway?"

"I took off to explore one day—I suppose I should have told someone where I was going, but I was in a rush. And Annabelle, your parents didn't like me to talk about my explorations. So I just dashed to the attic, and I was so close, *so* close, to *Amaurobius ferox*. I could just see her legs creeping out from under a floorboard when someone came into the attic with a big pile of things. Boxes and clothing and I don't know what. I didn't even know anyone was at home. I hid right away, of course. Whoever it was was very busy for quite a while—putting things away, moving cartons around. I thought I had found the perfect hiding place when suddenly I felt the trunk shift, and then it was lifted up slightly, and when it was lowered to the ground it came down on my dress. It just missed my legs and my left arm. I was lucky it hadn't come down on me—I would have been crushed—but I was trapped. I couldn't move. I thought I would just wait for some kind of help to come, and then I suppose I must have drifted off."

"For forty-five years!" exclaimed Tiffany. "Isn't that something?"

"Forty-five years," Auntie Sarah repeated. "Why Katherine must be . . . let me see . . ."

"She's a grandmother now," said Tiffany.

"She had a daughter named Annie," added Annabelle. "Named for me, I think, and now Annie has a daughter named Kate, and we are Kate's dolls."

"Well, I'm not," said Tiffany. "I'm one of Nora's dolls."

"Who's Nora?" asked Auntie Sarah.

So Annabelle and Tiffany sat down to tell Auntie Sarah some of the things that had happened since she had disappeared. They were trying to explain about the Funcrafts' dream house when suddenly Annabelle cried, "Tiffany! What are we doing? We have to go home! Now. And we have to figure out some way to get Auntie Sarah out of here."

"We're going to need help," said Tiffany.

"I know." Annabelle paused. Then she said, "I just thought of something. What will we do with Auntie Sarah after we free her? We can't just bring her back to our house after all these years. She can't simply appear there. What would the Palmers think?"

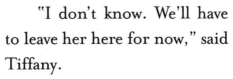 "I don't know. We'll have to leave her here for now," said Tiffany.

 Annabelle gazed down at Auntie Sarah. "I finally find you and now I have to leave you . . . in this place?" She looked around the dim, dusty attic and almost let out a sob.

"We don't have a choice," said Tiffany. "I already heard the clock chime four. Come *on*, Annabelle."

She grabbed Annabelle's

hand, and Annabelle said desperately, "We'll be back as soon as we can, Auntie Sarah. I promise. So long for now!" she called over her shoulder as Tiffany pulled her toward the stairs.

When Annabelle scrambled back up the stool and into the Dolls' house later, she was so excited that all she managed to blurt out was, "We found Auntie Sarah!"

"You found her? You actually found her?" cried Mama Doll.

"Yes, and she's alive."

Papa sat down heavily in a chair, Nanny gasped, and Annabelle thought that this time Uncle Doll was going to faint. But he didn't.

"We must go to the attic and get her immediately," he said, and it was only later that Annabelle would realize she hadn't yet said *where* she and Tiffany had found Auntie Sarah. In the excitement, though, no one else noticed.

The Dolls asked a million questions, and Annabelle answered them proudly. But after just a few minutes, Annabelle said, "You know, we have a big problem. I don't think it's going to be too difficult to rescue Auntie Sarah. I think if we all go to the attic together we can work her dress out from under the trunk. But then . . . then what are we going to *do* with her?"

No one spoke. Annabelle knew it was on the tip of everyone's tongue to say, "Why, just bring her home, of course," but each of the Dolls stopped upon realizing that that was exactly the kind of thing that would put them in jeopardy.

Eventually, the Dolls had to resume their positions before a plan had been made, but Annabelle whispered, just as the alarm clock went off, "We'll meet with the Funcrafts tonight. I know we'll figure something out."

The next day the Dolls were less careful than usual. Whenever they thought they were alone they scurried into the parlor to talk about Auntie Sarah. But by nightfall they had decided on only one thing: that when the Funcrafts came over, Nanny would stay behind with Baby Britney and Baby Betsy, and the rest of the dolls would go to the attic to see Auntie Sarah.

Annabelle was terrified that something would happen to keep them from making the trip up the attic stairs—that The Captain would appear, or that it would begin to rain again, or even that Kate would have trouble sleeping. But none of those things happened. And shortly before midnight, Annabelle found herself leading the way up the stairs. Behind her she could hear all sorts of groans and grunts and exclamations. Mama and Papa had particular difficulty with the steps, but Mom and Dad Funcraft helped them.

"Isn't this exciting?" Annabelle whispered to Tiffany as they neared the top step. "Look what SELMP has done!"

"We are amazing," said Tiffany.

The moment the last of the rescuers— Papa—had huffed and puffed his way up the top step, the nine dolls looked ahead of them into the dimly lit room.

"This is the gateway to the attic," said Tiffany dramatically.

"Where's Auntie Sarah?" asked Uncle Doll.

"Over here," said Annabelle, and led the way to the trunk.

"Look at all this *stuff*," exclaimed Bobby as they passed by the boxes and crates and old odd pieces of furniture.

"We definitely have to come back here," said Bailey. "We could play here every night. Think what we might find."

"It's quite a playground," agreed Mom Funcraft.

Mama and Papa said little, but Annabelle could see them gazing around the attic with wide, curious eyes.

"Okay, Auntie Sarah is back here," Annabelle finally announced. "Come on, everybody."

Just then, Papa held out a hand. "Uncle Doll should go first," he said quietly.

So Annabelle led Uncle Doll around the corner of the trunk and then slipped back to her family and the Funcrafts. She wanted to listen to what was being said between Uncle Doll and Auntie Sarah, but Mama shook her head.

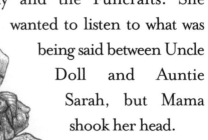

Finally, after several minutes had passed, Papa said, "All right. Now I think the rest of us would like to see Auntie Sarah."

"Okay," said Annabelle, and she walked around the trunk again, this time followed by the other dolls. "Here she is," she said.

And there was Auntie Sarah, still lying on the floor, of course, but now Uncle Doll was kneeling beside her, holding her hand.

"I just can't believe I've been here for forty-five years," Auntie Sarah was saying. "I feel like Rip Van Winkle."

"Who's Rip Van Winkle?" Bailey asked, but in the confusion that followed, no one answered him.

Annabelle introduced Auntie Sarah to the Funcrafts, and then all the grown-up Dolls began talking at once. Mostly Annabelle heard apologies—from Mama and Papa and Uncle Doll. And then she heard Mama say something she would have to ask her about later. "We thought you had run away."

Run away? "Why—" Annabelle started to say.

But Mom Funcraft had stepped over to Uncle Doll, who was still holding Auntie Sarah's hand. "I know you haven't seen each other in a very long time," she said to Auntie Sarah, "but shouldn't we see if we can't free your dress?"

Uncle Doll answered for her. "Oh, my. Yes. Of course! How silly of us." He got to his feet.

Mama and Papa and Uncle Doll and Mom and Dad examined Auntie Sarah's dress and the trunk.

"If we all work together, could we move the trunk?" asked Bobby from behind them.

"I don't think so," replied Papa after a moment.

"But if we work together, I believe we can pull Sarah's dress out from under it," said Uncle Doll.

The dolls, all nine of them, bent down next to Auntie Sarah and each grabbed two handfuls of her dress.

They pulled.

They pulled harder.

They braced their feet against the trunk and groaned and pulled even harder.

"Hey! It's moving!" cried Bailey.

And so it was. Very slowly, Auntie Sarah's dress was sliding out from under the trunk where it had been trapped for forty-five years. In the end, a small piece caught on the brass fixture on the corner and tore off, but it was so tiny, and Auntie Sarah was already so very dirty and dusty and cobwebby, that Annabelle didn't think it would matter.

Auntie Sarah raised her hands to her head. "Goodness," she said. "Thank you." Uncle Doll helped her to sit up, which she did stiffly.

Then she announced that she felt fit as a fiddle and ready to go, but Uncle Doll held her back. "Not yet," he said. "We haven't

figured out what to do with you. You can't just appear in Kate's dollhouse. That would raise suspicions."

"It certainly would," said Mama.

"But luckily, I have an idea," said Annabelle.

"You do?" said Tiffany. "You didn't tell me."

"I just thought of it now," replied Annabelle. "What we must do is get Auntie Sarah to a place where one of the Palmers will find her so she can be returned to the dollhouse by a human. That wouldn't put us in jeopardy. So I thought: Where could she go after all these years that won't make the Palmers suspicious? Right away it came to me—The Captain's bed! If we put Auntie Sarah there, the Palmers will think The Captain has been prowling around again and *he* found Auntie Sarah somewhere and took her to his bed so he could play with her."

"That's brilliant!" exclaimed Tiffany, and everyone agreed.

Except for Auntie Sarah, who simply said, "Who's The Captain?"

Annabelle explained and after a moment Auntie Sarah said, "A cat's bed? . . . Well, all right. If I must, I must. Let's go."

"Oh, not tonight, Sarah," said Uncle Doll. "I'm afraid there isn't enough time. We'll have to go tomorrow."

"You mean I have to spend another night in the attic?" said Auntie Sarah. "Oh, dear. Well, perhaps I'll see *Amaurobius ferox* after all. Or even *Araneus diadematus*. What a shame I don't have my journal with me."

The dolls talked for a bit longer and then

Papa said to Auntie Sarah, "It's time for us to leave. I'm terribly sorry. But we'll be back tomorrow night."

"And maybe by the day after that, you'll be home again," said Annabelle.

CHAPTER SEVENTEEN

The Captain Helps Out

NNABELLE Doll put her hand to her mouth and gasped. Once again, she had led the rest of the dolls to the attic and now she was standing in the spot where Auntie Sarah had been trapped for so long—and Auntie Sarah wasn't there.

"She's gone!" Annabelle cried softly.

"Oh, again?" said Uncle Doll.

"No! No! I'm here. I'm right here." Auntie Sarah came bustling out from under a footstool. "I thought I saw a fine male specimen of *Philodromus dispar* run under here, but I guess not. I can't find him anywhere."

"Thank goodness," Annabelle muttered to Tiffany.

"Are you ready to go downstairs, Sarah?" asked Mama.

"To be discovered?" added Mom Funcraft.

"I've never been so ready," replied Auntie Sarah.

"All right, then. Let's go." This time Papa led the way back to the attic stairs.

"Mama, can Bailey and I stay in the attic and play?" asked Bobby.

"Not tonight, dear. We have an important job to do."

"We have a *mission*," Tiffany whispered to Annabelle.

"Well, can we come back tomorrow?"

"We'll see."

"Bobby, come *on*," said Annabelle. "If you're not going to take this seriously, then you should have stayed home with Nanny and the babies."

"Children, that's enough," said Mama. "No arguing."

As the dolls neared the bottom of the stairs, Annabelle began explaining things to

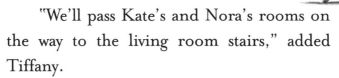

Auntie Sarah. "Now, in case you don't remember, the door just to the right is where the parents sleep. Only now the parents are Annie and her husband. Grandma Katherine's room is down-stairs."

"We'll pass Kate's and Nora's rooms on the way to the living room stairs," added Tiffany.

"And once we're on the first floor, we should keep an eye out for The Captain," said Annabelle. "I don't know where he stays now at night, and he's very crafty."

But the Dolls and the Funcrafts, with Annabelle, Tiffany, and Auntie Sarah in the lead, made their way to the living room without running into any humans or The Captain. Annabelle breathed a sigh of relief.

"All right. Now where is The Captain's b—?" Auntie Sarah started to ask. She paused as she looked around the living room. "My, everything is so different. The furniture has been moved. No, wait. It isn't even the same furniture. And where is the radio?"

"The Palmers don't listen to the radio much," said Bobby. "Mostly they watch TV."

Of course Auntie Sarah didn't know what TV was, even when Annabelle and Tiffany showed her the big TV that now sat where the radio had once stood.

"Maybe someone will turn it on while you're waiting in The Captain's bed," said Bailey. "Then you can see what it is."

"It's sort of like a radio with moving pictures," Tiffany added helpfully. But Auntie Sarah said she couldn't envision it.

"Well, anyway, here's the bed," said Tiffany, taking Auntie Sarah by the hand and pulling her to the horrible old sweater behind the armchair. "I'm sorry it's so hairy."

Uncle Doll put his arm around Auntie Sarah. "You probably won't have to stay here for long," he said.

But suddenly Annabelle felt a prickle of alarm. "Oh, no . . ."

"What, Annabelle?" said Papa.

"What if The Captain finds Auntie Sarah and takes her out of his bed and runs away with her? He might not play with her in his bed, you know. Or what if none of the humans looks in the bed for a long, long time? Oh, why didn't we think of these things earlier? This was a stupid idea."

"Ahem. You forget whom you're talking about," said Auntie Sarah. "If the humans don't look here soon, I'll think of something. As for The Captian, well, I've not met him, of course, but I have no doubt I could escape from him. And when I do, I'll just come back here to his bed. I'm not afraid of cats, you know."

Mom Funcraft smiled at her. "We find that cats can be a wonderful source of exercise."

"Not to mention that they are fascinating to study," said Auntie Sarah. "Now, go on back to your houses, all of you. I'll be fine down here. With any luck, I'll see the TV before I come home. I'm certain I'll be back in a day or two."

The Dolls and the Funcrafts said hasty good-byes to Auntie Sarah. They were in their homes long before the Palmers awoke. For a while Annabelle sat on her bed and thought about her aunt. She thought about finding her trapped in the attic. Then she thought about the day so long ago when Auntie Sarah had disappeared.

"Mama?" said Annabelle, sliding into a chair in the kitchen where her mother was sitting at the table.

Mama Doll looked up from the bit of sewing she sometimes worked on at night. "Yes?"

"Mama, I heard you say something to Auntie Sarah when we were in the attic last night, and I didn't understand it."

"What was it?" asked Mama.

"You said, 'We thought you had run away.' What did you mean?"

Mama Doll put down her sewing. "Well . . ."

"Why would Auntie Sarah run away from us?" Annabelle continued. "Didn't she love us?"

"Oh, yes. Of course she loved us. But she was so . . . different from the rest of us. She was so much more bold. And we were—"

"Timid?" Annabelle suggested.

"Not timid, exactly. Careful. We have to be careful, Annabelle. You know that. And we felt that Auntie Sarah wanted to take chances. Sometimes that led to arguments. Auntie Sarah thought we were holding her back from things she wanted to do, and we thought

Auntie Sarah was putting us in danger. So when she disappeared—"

Annabelle interrupted again. "When she disappeared you thought she had run away."

"Yes."

"You thought she *wanted* to leave us."

"Which was a horrible thought, of course."

"So *that's* why you didn't look for her. You thought she didn't want to be found."

"Partly. And partly we were afraid to look. We felt terrible. Uncle Doll wanted to look for her. *He* wasn't sure she had run away. But Papa and Nanny and I were. And anyway, we never, ever left the house on our own."

Annabelle felt a tremendous sense of relief, as if something very heavy had been lifted from her heart. "So if I *did* disappear, you *would* come look- ing for me? Even if

you were a little afraid? I mean, if you thought something awful had happened and I wouldn't be returned by Kate or someone in a few days?"

"Oh, yes. Yes, of course, Annabelle."

Annabelle leaned forward and hugged her mother.

The next day Annabelle was in a frenzy of contained excitement. How could she just sit in her house waiting for someone to walk into Kate's room holding Auntie Sarah? Especially when that might not happen for days and days? Annabelle knew she was impatient but, she thought, anyone would be impatient in this situation. She could tell that even her parents and

Uncle Doll and Nanny were having trouble behaving like dolls. While Kate was still in her room getting ready for school, the adults would shift their eyes toward the door if they heard the slightest noise in the hall. And the moment Kate left, Uncle Doll sat up from his place on the kitchen floor and said, "Oh, agony!" which made Annabelle and Bobby laugh.

It was shortly before noon that day, when the house was very quiet and only Grandma Katherine was at home, that the Dolls heard a shriek.

"Oh, my stars!" Grandma Katherine cried from the living room. Immediately, the Dolls heard her footsteps on the stairs. Annabelle crossed her fingers behind her back.

"I'll be," said Grandma Katherine a moment later as she bustled into Kate's room. "After all these years. I wonder where The Captain found you."

Annabelle had been left in an awkward position on the floor next to the icebox, but she had a good view of the door to Kate's room. She watched as Grandma Katherine hurried to the Dolls' house with Auntie Sarah cupped in one hand.

"Won't Annie and Kate be surprised," muttered Grandma Katherine. As she spoke, she dusted off Auntie Sarah's clothes, and polished her arms and legs and face on the edge of her blouse. Then she clucked over the tear in her dress. "Why, your hand is chipped," she said. "Actually, you're quite a mess. Poor Auntie Sarah."

Grandma Katherine fussed over Auntie Sarah some more, straightening and brushing and adjusting and wiping. "There," she said finally. "That's better. Although I don't think I can do much about your dress." She sat Auntie Sarah on the couch in the parlor. "My goodness. Annie and Kate have never seen you," she continued. "I think I'll just let Kate find you here and see what she says."

Grandma Katherine stood back and gazed at the sight of Auntie Sarah, back in the dollhouse where she belonged. Then she hurried out of the room, a smile on her face.

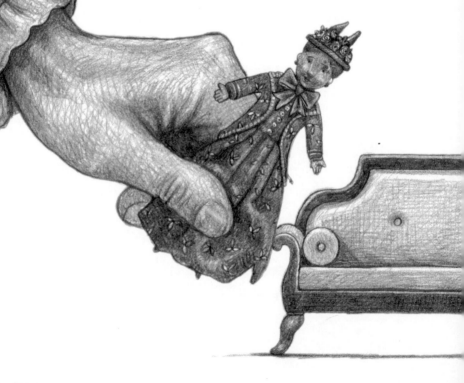

The Dolls waited patiently. When they could no longer hear her footsteps on the stairs, they rushed to Auntie Sarah and surrounded her once again in a hug.

"We ought to have a celebration of some sort," said Mama in a whisper.

"We ought to have a double celebration," said Auntie Sarah. "Annabelle's birthday is in three days."

Leave it to Auntie Sarah to remember something like that after all this time. Annabelle gazed at her aunt and decided she was one of the most wonderful people in the world.

CHAPTER EIGHTEEN

Annabelle's Birthday Party

THE NEXT few days were a whirl of activity for Annabelle and her family. The Palmers kept visiting the dollhouse to exclaim over Auntie Sarah. And of course all the Dolls wanted to spend time with her, to hear of her adventures, of getting stuck under the trunk, about her night in The Captain's bed. And they wanted to tell Auntie Sarah the events of the last forty-five years. There was so much talking to be done that no one was as careful as usual about when they moved around or where the humans were or who was at home. But they were careful enough, and no one got caught.

At night, the Dolls and the Funcrafts ran back and forth between their houses, planning the party. It was to be held at the Funcrafts', since the Dolls still had not had a proper visit to their home, had only seen it from a distance. Tiffany told Annabelle to expect a little surprise, but she wouldn't say anything more than that.

On the night of the party, the Dolls waited until the stroke of midnight before they began the climb down the stool. Annabelle had insisted on that. It wasn't her birthday until midnight, not really, and she didn't want the adventure to begin until her birthday had begun as well.

Annabelle watched as her family made their way down the hallway to Nora's room, Mama holding a fresh bouquet of paper flowers. Uncle Doll and Auntie Sarah were in the lead, and Annabelle was proud of her brave uncle. He held Auntie Sarah's hand, and talked quietly with her.

When the Dolls reached Nora's doorway, Annabelle peeked around the corner. "Here we are again," she whispered.

Bailey waved to them from the doorway.
"Hey, everybody!" he called. "Happy birthday, Annabelle! Come on in!"

Annabelle darted across Nora's floor,

her family following. She ran straight to
Tiffany and together they entered the
Funcrafts' house. Annabelle drew in her
breath, ready to say how lovely, how charm-

ing the decor was. Instead she found herself saying, "My, how . . . how modern."

"Thanks," replied Tiffany.

Annabelle gazed around. Everything in
the house was plastic and most of it was pink.
And it was still a huge mess. Furniture, books,
pots and pans—everything that had come with
the house was in a jumble. Chairs were tossed
in corners. Tables were overturned. Pots and
pans were scattered about the floor. The
kitchen sink was resting on the staircase.

"I guess Nora hasn't finished setting up
your house yet," Annabelle said to Tiffany.

"It isn't that so much," Tiffany replied.
"She never even started to set it up. But she
plays in the house almost every day, and she
just tosses things around. Yesterday, for
instance, she was giving Baby Britney rides
through the house in the flying sink."

Annabelle caught sight of a hideous plastic chicken and a dusting of powder in the
dining room and thought she knew what else
Nora had been doing.

The rest of the Dolls had now entered the
house. Mama presented the flowers to Mom
Funcraft, who was delighted by them, and

fussed about, looking for a vase. Annabelle saw that Baby Betsy and Baby Britney were seated facing each other on the kitchen floor. Baby Betsy was nearly twice as tall as Baby Britney, but neither one seemed to mind. Bailey was leading Bobby upstairs. Dad Funcraft was showing Papa and Uncle Doll the microwave. Mom was showing the computer to Mama and Nanny.

"Do you have your own room?" Annabelle asked Tiffany.

"It depends," Tiffany replied.

"On what?"

"On where Nora puts our furniture. I'm supposed to share a room with Bailey and Baby Britney, but right now Bailey's bed is on the patio, and the crib is up on the roof. So I guess I have the room to myself. Do you want to see it?"

"Oh, yes," replied Annabelle.

Tiffany and Annabelle ran up the stairs and into what Annabelle supposed was a bedroom. She supposed this because a bed lay upside down in a corner of the room. But she did not see a dresser or a rug or anything else that was in the nursery at the Dolls' house.

Instead she saw two plastic sheep, a couch, a box of Tide, and a dining room chair.

Annabelle and Tiffany sat together on the couch.

"I'll tell you a secret," Tiffany offered. "One day—this was quite a while ago— The Captain was bothering me. Usually I like him, but this one time he was really being a pain in the neck."

"Yes?" said Annabelle.

"Well, he was in the closet, so I pushed the door closed. I shut him in! He was only stuck there for a few minutes before Nora heard him scratching and let him out. But he learned his lesson."

"Goodness," said Annabelle, impressed. She thought for a moment, then said, "I know a secret too."

"You do? What is it?"

"I think I know who was writing in Auntie Sarah's journal."

Tiffany's mouth dropped open. "Who?" she cried.

"I can't tell you yet. I have to talk to the person first."

"But after you do that, will you tell me?"

"Definitely."

Annabelle found that she couldn't stop smiling. Suddenly there were a million things she wanted to tell Tiffany, old secrets she wanted to share with her. But Annabelle decided to keep the most important secret of all to herself. The secret was this: she believed she had found a true friend, a doll friend. Auntie Sarah was back and Annabelle loved her, but she was a grown-up. Annabelle loved Kate, too, but Kate was a human. Tiffany was a doll girl her own age. Annabelle realized she no longer felt restless. And she no longer felt that something was missing. She had found Tiffany and she felt whole.

And she was fairly certain that with

Tiffany around she would never be bored again.

The doll friends talked in Tiffany's room for a long time. They talked until they heard Mom Funcraft call from downstairs.

"Tiffany! Bailey! Annabelle! Bobby! Dinner's ready!"

Annabelle leaped to her feet, pulling Tiffany up behind her.

The dolls gathered on the Funcrafts' patio, which was only slightly sticky with the remnants of the grape soda. In the center of the patio was a stand on top of which was a brown plastic box with a lid.

"What's that?" asked Annabelle, pointing.

"The barbecue," replied Tiffany.

"Oh. The great taste of outdoors," said Annabelle, remembering. She walked closer for a better look. "Does it really work?"

"No. It just opens and closes."

Presently, the party was under way. Baby Betsy and Baby Britney sat on a blanket, playing with the pink plastic pots and pans. Mom Funcraft and Mama Doll chatted and set the

table while Dad Funcraft
and Papa Doll bustled back
and forth between the
kitchen and the patio, carrying trays of dishes and
cups and plastic food.

"Okay, dig in, every-
body," said Mom Funcraft.

The Dolls and the
Funcrafts oohed and ahhed
over the feast that was
before them.

Then Annabelle followed Tiffany's lead and gathered up a plate, a cup, and a checked napkin. She sat on the edge of the patio with the plate balanced on her knees, and pretended to eat. Annabelle had never eaten a meal from her lap, and she thought it was fun.

When the meal was over, Mom Funcraft said, "All right. Tiffany and Bailey will collect the plates now, and then they will help me with something in the kitchen. The rest of you wait here."

Annabelle watched Tiffany help her

mother and brother. Then she sat back and waited. She had the delicious feeling that something nice was about to happen. And she was right.

A few minutes later, Tiffany walked onto the patio holding a pink plastic cake in front of her. Bailey and Mom Funcraft were behind her, and they began to sing. The others joined in. They sang two verses. First they sang, "Happy birthday to you, happy birthday to you, happy birthday, dear Annabelle, happy birthday to you!" Then they sang, "Welcome home and welcome back, welcome home and welcome back, welcome ho-ome, Auntie Sarah, welcome home and welcome back!"

Tiffany set the cake on a table between Annabelle and Auntie Sarah. "I'm sorry we can't put candles on it to make it a real birthday cake," she said. "They won't stick to the plastic, and besides, we don't have any matches. But you can still make a birthday wish. A secret one, okay? You make a secret wish, too, Auntie Sarah. Just close your eyes and think your wishes."

Annabelle closed her eyes. She thought, I

am the luckiest doll alive. Papa came home safe and sound. Then Auntie Sarah came home safe and sound. I've just had my first real birthday party ever. *And* I have a friend. I don't need a birthday wish. I only want to say thank you. This has been the best birthday in a hundred years.

After the cake, Tiffany and Bailey put on a program of songs and skits, and then everybody sang "Under the Boardwalk." After that, it was time for the Dolls to go home.

"What an evening," said Papa as they reached their house.

"How wonderful to have neighbors," added Mama. "How did we manage to live for a century without them?"

"I don't know," said Annabelle, thinking of her new friend.

"They're so very . . . odd," said Uncle Doll slowly, "and yet—"

"And yet amazing," said Bobby.

"Adventurous," said Auntie Sarah.

"Very friendly," said Nanny.

"And neighborly," agreed Papa.

"But mostly friendly," said Annabelle.

The Dolls were gathering in the parlor

when Annabelle pulled Uncle Doll aside and whispered to him, "Could I talk to you for a minute?"

"Of course."

Annabelle and her uncle sat at the kitchen table.

"I want to ask you something," said Annabelle.

"Yes?" replied Uncle Doll.

Annabelle watched him fidgeting and thought that Uncle Doll already had an idea what her question was.

"Did you know that I had found Auntie Sarah's journal, and were you the one who started writing in it?" she asked.

Uncle Doll rested his hands on the table. "Yes," he said quietly.

"You were giving me clues, weren't you? Clues that would lead Tiffany and me to the attic."

"Yes."

"Did you know all along that Auntie Sarah was there?"

"No," replied Uncle Doll. "I wasn't sure what had happened to her. But I had an idea that if she were stuck somewhere it might be the attic. Then you found the journal and I started reading it. When I got to the parts about the spiders, well . . ."

Annabelle thought for a moment before asking her next question. "Why didn't *you* go to the attic?" she said finally.

"Me?" said Uncle Doll. "I—I suppose I could have, but you . . . and Tiffany . . . I don't know."

Annabelle knew, though. She knew what her uncle was trying to say. He had been afraid. Truly afraid. But he had thought Annabelle and Tiffany were brave enough and adventurous enough to do the job. He just hadn't known quite how to ask them to do it. And perhaps he hadn't wanted Annabelle to know how afraid he really was.

He was starting to change, though, now, a little. But Annabelle realized just how different she and Auntie Sarah were from Uncle Doll and Mama and Papa and Nanny. And suddenly, breathlessly, she felt flattered. She even felt a bit like a grown-up, which was both scary and wonderful.

"Uncle Doll," Annabelle said, straightening herself, "why is it that I don't remember Auntie Sarah leaving our house to go exploring?"

"Well, for one thing, she didn't go very often," he replied. "And when she did go, your parents insisted that she do it secretly, that you and Bobby never know she had left. She would climb out the window in our bedroom and drop to the little carpet below. There used to be a rug under our house," he added. "When she returned, Nanny made sure you and Bobby were engaged, that you didn't see her."

"But why didn't Mama and Papa want Bobby and me to know about Auntie Sarah's adventures? Was it because they thought we would want to leave too?"

"Yes," replied Uncle Doll. "And they felt that was too dangerous."

"And now?" said Annabelle. "What do they think now?"

"They still think that leaving the house can be dangerous. After all, look what has happened when we *have* left our house. Sarah was lost for forty-five years. Your father was carried off by a cat. But I think your parents understand that some doll people—you and Sarah, for instance—*need* to leave the house. You are unhappy when you're cooped up. I believe they'll continue to let you leave as long as you're careful. They want you to be happy, Annabelle. And so do I."

"I know," replied Annabelle. "Thank you."

She took Uncle Doll's hand in hers and they sat quietly in the kitchen for a while.

Grandma Katherine and the Dolls

AFTER THE party at the Funcrafts', Annabelle and Tiffany saw each other nearly every night, and sometimes during the day.

"If Nora had gotten Funcraft Dream House model *two*-ten," Tiffany said to Annabelle one morning, "I would have come with a friendship necklace."

"What's a friendship necklace?" Annabelle asked. She and Tiffany were sitting on the edge of Tiffany's bedroom, their legs dangling over the side of the dream house.

"Well, it's actually two necklaces," Tiffany

replied. "Hanging from each one is half of a broken heart. If you put the pieces together you have one whole heart, with the words BEST FRIENDS on it. If I gave you one of the necklaces, that would mean you were my best friend. And that is what I would do if I had a friendship necklace."

Annabelle beamed.

And any time afterward, when Annabelle remembered Tiffany's words, she felt tingly all over.

One evening, a Wednesday, Annabelle, who had been draped over the back of a kitchen chair, waiting impatiently for Kate to turn out her light and go to sleep, heard Grandma Katherine's voice in the hallway.

"Kate?" she said. "Darling? You aren't asleep yet, are you?"

"No," replied Kate, who was reading in the glow of her bedside lamp. Annabelle thought she was reading *Understood Betsy*, but she wasn't sure. And she didn't dare turn her head to see.

Grandma Katherine walked slowly into Kate's room and sat on the edge of her bed.

"Hi," said Kate.

"Hi." Grandma Katherine tilted Kate's book so she could see the title. "Oh. I remember reading that with your mother."

"When she was eight?" asked Kate.

"Yes. When she was eight. Are you enjoying the book?"

"Yes. But I'm having trouble concentrating on it right now."

"You are? Why?"

"I'm thinking about something else," replied Kate. "Something I've been thinking about a lot lately."

"And what is that?" asked Grandma Katherine.

"The dolls."

"The dolls? Annabelle and Bobby and the dolls in the dollhouse?"

"Yes. Especially Auntie Sarah."

"It's nice to have her back, isn't it? The dolls are very special, Kate. Did you know I named your mother Annie because of Annabelle?"

"I thought you might have. But I wasn't sure," said Kate.

"What is it that you've been thinking about the dolls?"

Kate drew in a deep breath. She let it out. "Grandma Katherine," she said at last, "did you ever think the dolls are alive?"

Grandma Katherine smiled. "Well, I did wonder about that when I was your age."

"And what do you think now?" asked Kate.

Grandma Katherine hesitated. "Sometimes I still wonder."

Kate lifted her head, and her grandmother turned around so that they were both gazing into the Dolls' house.

Annabelle, still draped over the kitchen chair, didn't move. But she smiled to herself.

Ann M. Martin is the author of the Newbery Honor Book, *A Corner of the Universe*, as well as many other books for young readers, including *The Meanest Doll in the World*, the sequel to *The Doll People*, cowritten with Laura Godwin and illustrated by Brian Selznick. She is also the coauthor, with Paula Danziger, of *P.S. Longer Letter Later* and *Snail Mail No More*. Ms. Martin funds such charities as The Lisa Libraries and The Ann M. Martin Foundation. She makes her home in upstate New York.

Laura Godwin, also known as Nola Buck, is the author of many popular picture books for children, including *Barnyard Prayers*, illustrated by Brian Selznick; *The Flower Girl*, illustrated by John Wallace; *Little White Dog*, illustrated by Dan Yaccarino; *Christmas in the Manger*, illustrated by Felicia Bond; and *Central Park Serenade*, illustrated by Barry Root. Born and raised in Alberta, Canada, she now lives in New York City.

Brian Selznick received the Caldecott Honor for *The Dinosaurs of Waterhouse Hawkins* by Barbara Kerley. He is also the illustrator of *Wingwalker* by Rosemary Wells; *Frindle* by Andrew Clements; and *Amelia and Eleanor Go for a Ride* and *When Marian Sang*, both by Pam Muñoz Ryan. He also wrote and illustrated *The Boy of a Thousand Faces* and *The Houdini Box*, the latter the winner of the Texas Bluebonnet Award. Mr. Selznick lives in Brooklyn, New York.

FUNCRAFT
Dream House™
Model 110
Made by Marwin Incorporated

WARNING:
CHOKING HAZARD:
small parts.
Not for children
under 3 years.

Some assembly required.

Use these instructions to assemble your
FUNCRAFT Dream House™ Model 110.

TO ASSEMBLE Dream House™:

1. Slide second floor into place (fig. 1).
2. Attach pillars and walls through second floor (fig. 2).

3. Snap on patio (fig. 3).
4. Snap on stairs and
   barbecue as shown
   (fig. 4).

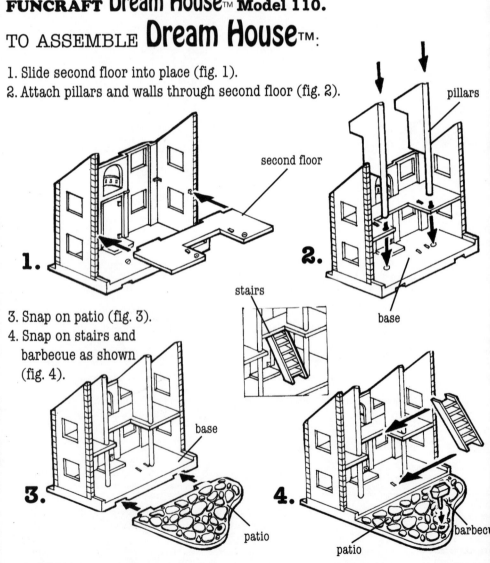

second floor

pillars

1.

2.

stairs

base

base

3.

patio

4.

patio

barbecu

barbecu

REAL PINK PLASTIC

Ages 5 and up

5. Attach roof (fig. 5).

roof

5.

6. Your DREAM HOUSE™ is now complete! Congratulations! you are ready to move in.

Here is your Funcraft Family

1. Dad   **2.** Mom   **3.** Tiffany   **4.** Bailey   **5.** Baby Britney

Marwin: The name you think of when you think of fun! We guarantee all Funcraft products. Made with famous patented Flexy-Bendy™ arms and legs, *the limbs that lead to laughs!*™ Rated top non-toxic toy for tots in *Plastic World* magazine. All Funcraft heads rated 100% unremovable in *Rough Kid* magazine. "It's *so* pink!" says child star Aurora Bow. . . . Have a question? Call our Dream House hotline right away. 1-800-Marwin1

Annabelle and Tiffany's adventures continue in

THE MEANEST DOLL
IN THE WORLD

CHAPTER THREE

A Close Call

EVEN THOUGH GOING down the stairs was easier than going up, the dolls had to take their time. The attic stairs were not carpeted, so Annabelle and Tiffany and Auntie Sarah moved quietly and cautiously. Every time Annabelle looked at the floor below, she couldn't help but worry what would happen if she were to slip and fall the rest of the way down. She didn't mention this, though, as brave Auntie Sarah and Tiffany scrambled ahead of her.

When they reached the bottom, Annabelle peered around the door. "It must be later than we think," she whispered. "There's a lot of light in the hallway."

"Hmm. By my calculations it couldn't be later than five o'clock," said Auntie Sarah.

"Five o'clock!" exclaimed Annabelle. "We were supposed to be home by four. Mama and Papa—"

Tiffany gave Annabelle a little push into the hall. "Well, let's not waste time talking about it," she said. "Hurry up. Run!"

Annabelle and Tiffany ran into the hallway ahead of Auntie Sarah. They had just passed Nora's room when Annabelle screeched to a halt and let out a small shriek.

"What's wrong?" asked Tiffany.

"I heard something!"

And at that moment, Annabelle, staring ahead of her, saw a pair of bare feet step from Kate's room into the hall. She almost shrieked again, but Tiffany clapped a hand over her mouth. Annabelle looked wildly around. Auntie Sarah had ducked back behind the attic door. Annabelle could see her shoes beneath it. The door to Kate's room was a few feet ahead. On the floor

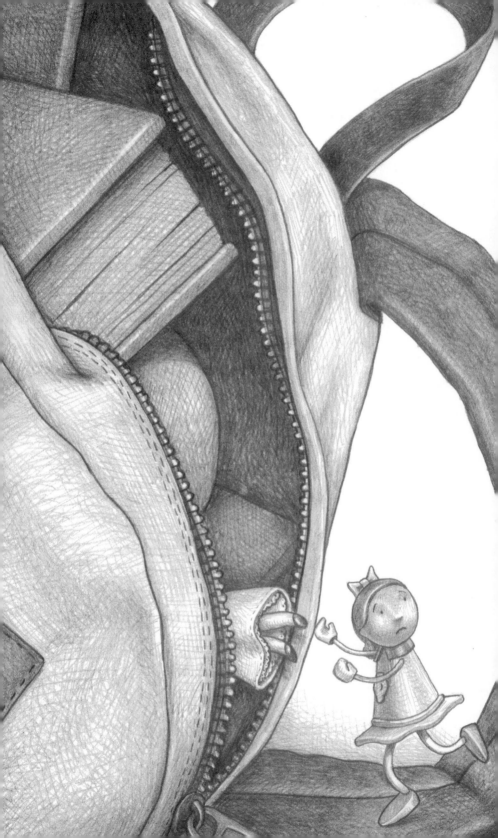

outside of it, just inches from the dolls, was Kate's backpack.

"Quick!" said Tiffany in a loud whisper. "The attic!"

"No, she'll see us!" Annabelle saw Tiffany's eyes jump hopefully to Nora's doorway. "We can't go there either," said Annabelle. She was feeling panicky. The bare feet were moving sleepily along the hallway, closer and closer. In a flash Annabelle grabbed Tiffany by the wrist and yanked her toward the backpack. "In here," she said.

Annabelle dove headfirst into the largest compartment of the backpack with Tiffany just behind her. She tried not to squeal as she sat on something sharp, then felt Tiffany land on her head. The girls huddled together, breathing heavily and listening to the sounds from the hallway. They heard Kate's footsteps pad into the bathroom. Then the bathroom door was closed gently.

"Safe!" exclaimed Tiffany softly. "That was a close call. Good thinking, Annabelle."

"Thank you. I hope Auntie Sarah saw us hide in here," Annabelle whispered. She frowned. "How on earth could she have made such a mistake? If Kate is already up it must be much later than five."

"Well, we can't worry about that now," replied Tiffany. "We have to figure out what to do. Do you think we have time to get out of here?"

Annabelle didn't have a chance to answer. The girls heard the bathroom door open again. "Okay, as soon as Kate goes back to her room," Tiffany said quickly, "we'll climb out and run into Nora's room. She's probably still asleep. You can hide with my family, and we'll just have to hope Kate won't notice you're missing from—"

"Shh," hissed Annabelle suddenly. "Shh, SHH!"

Tiffany stopped talking as a hand appeared above the backpack and with a loud Z-I-I-I-P, closed it up, leaving Annabelle and Tiffany in darkness. Annabelle grabbed for Tiffany's hand and held it tightly. Then

the backpack was swooped into the air and
Annabelle felt Kate wrap her arms around it.
She and Tiffany bumped up and down as Kate
carried the backpack . . . where?

"Where are we going?" whispered
Tiffany.

"Shh," was all Annabelle
would reply.

A few seconds later
the backpack was dropped
to the floor. Annabelle
crashed against Tiffany,
but remained silent. The
girls listened hard. They
heard Kate's radio play-
ing. They heard drawers
opening and closing, and
small thumps and clatters as
Kate got ready for school.
And all the while Annabelle
hoped that the following things
would happen: that Kate would partially open the backpack, and that she would
then forget what she was doing, abandon it,
and go downstairs for breakfast, at which point
Annabelle and Tiffany would crawl out and go

to their homes. They would have to admit to their parents what had happened, of course, but since Annabelle held Auntie Sarah responsible, she wasn't too worried about this.

However, none of those things happened. Kate left the backpack closed, and presently she slung it up again and carried it downstairs. With a small thump she deposited it on the floor. In the kitchen? In the hallway?

Kitchen, Annabelle decided as she heard clinkings and clankings and smelled toast and eggs. Annabelle wanted desperately to talk to Tiffany, but she knew better. It was a miracle that she and Tiffany weren't already in Doll State.

The clinkings and clankings grew louder, and Annabelle heard voices. Soon the entire Palmer family had gathered for breakfast. Just when the noise in the kitchen became so loud that Annabelle wanted to put her hands over her ears, she felt Tiffany nudge her. Annabelle

nudged
her back.
"Annabelle,"
Tiffany whispered
urgently.

"SHH!"

"Oh, they can't
hear us. Not with all
that racket. . . .
Annabelle?"

"What?"

"I'm sitting in gum."

"Gum? Are you sure?"

"Yes! I'm stuck in it. I can't
move."

Annabelle got to her feet carefully
and held out her hand to Tiffany. "Here.
Let me pull you up."

Tiffany took Annabelle's hand.
Annabelle pulled. And pulled. And pulled.
"I . . . can't . . . pull . . . any . . ." she said,
puffing, and at that moment, Tiffany suddenly flew toward her. The girls fell against
the edge of a book.

They hugged each other nervously, but all
they heard was the sound of chairs being

pushed back and voices calling good-bye as Kate's mother and father left for their jobs. And then . . . "Nora, hurry up!" called Kate as once again the backpack was lifted into the air.

Annabelle heard Grandma Katherine say, "Here, Kate. Let me help you with that," and she and Tiffany were jostled about as Kate struggled to put her arms through the straps of the backpack.

"Oh, there you are," said Kate a moment later. "Come on, Nora, we don't want to be late."

"Good-bye, girls," said Grandma Katherine. "See you later."

"Bye!" Kate and Nora called back.

A door closed, and Annabelle Doll was Outdoors.

She couldn't help whispering to Tiffany. "We're outdoors. *Outdoors*. I've never, ever been outdoors. I mean, not since our packing carton was delivered to Gertrude, and that was over a hundred years ago."

Tiffany gripped Annabelle's hand even harder. "I think we're going to *school*," she said.

To be continued . . .

Surrender, Annabelle